AUTOFICTI

Hitomi Kanehara was born in Tokyo on 8 August 1983. She stopped attending school at the age of eleven. After she left home as a teenager, she sent her stories by email to her literary translator father who helped her edit them. At the age of twenty-one she wrote *Snakes and Earrings* which won the 2004 Akutagawa Prize, the top Japanese literary award. One of the judges, the celebrated writer Ryu Murakami, said her book was 'easily the top choice, receiving the highest marks of any work since I became a member of the selection panel'. The Japanese edition of *Snakes and Earrings* has since sold over a million copies, topping all the bestseller lists. *Autofiction* is her second work to be published in English.

HITOMI KANEHARA

Autofiction

TRANSLATED FROM THE JAPANESE BY
David James Karashima

VINTAGE BOOKS
London

Published by Vintage 2007

10

Copyright © Hitomi Kanehara 2006
English translation copyright © David James Karashima 2007

Hitomi Kanehara has asserted her right under the Copyright, Designs and
Patents Act 1988 to be identified as the author of this work

First published in Japan by Shueisha Inc. in 2006

First published in Great Britain by Vintage in 2007

Vintage
Random House, 20 Vauxhall Bridge Road,
London SW1V 2SA

www.vintage-books.co.uk

Addresses for companies within The Random House Group Limited can
be found at: www.randomhouse.co.uk/offices.htm

The Random House Group Limited Reg. No. 954009

A CIP catalogue record for this book
is available from the British Library

ISBN 9780099515982

A VINTAGE ORIGINAL

Penguin Random House is committed to a sustainable future for
our business, our readers and our planet. This book is made from
Forest Stewardship Council® certified paper.

Typeset in Hiroshige Book by Palimpsest Book Production Limited,
Grangemouth, Stirlingshire
Printed and bound in Great Britain by Clays Ltd, Elcograf S.p.A

CONTENTS

1

22nd Winter

'Look! Look! It's amazing.'

'You're right. It really is.'

'Come on, though. Take a good look for yourself! See how amazing it is.'

'All right.'

'Wow!'

I take my pale fiancé's hand in mine and continue to stare out the window as our plane makes its steady ascent. I pray to the orange lights below me. Pray that next year he'll take me on another trip to celebrate our first wedding anniversary.

I don't want to go back to Japan. That's how wonderful our honeymoon in Tahiti had been. Anything and everything is just so much fun when the two of us are together. I close my eyes and try to etch the images from our time on the beach deep in my mind and I feel my hand getting damp from sweat. But it's not my hand that's sweating. It's his. He hates planes and he always turns pale during take-off and landing. Could he be any more adorable?

'Are you OK?'

'Yeah.'

'Your face is pale.'

'I know.'

As we speak, the plane shakes and he tightens his grip on my hand. So cute! My adorable husband! What a wonderful husband he is. His eyes are dead serious, trained on the altitude counter on the big screen. My eyes are dead serious, fixed only on him.

'What?' he turns to me and says.

'I love you,' I tell him, but his face turns slightly sour.

'How can you say that?' he says to me. 'At a time like this, when we could fall from the sky at any moment and die.'

Then he turns back to the big screen. His hand is soaked in sweat.

The only time I ever see him get scared is in a plane, so I keep my eyes glued on his face, determined to engrave this image in my mind. He's too preoccupied to stop me anyway.

'Would you like some champagne or juice?'

'Champagne,' he tells the Japanese stewardess who's suddenly appeared in front of us.

'Champagne, right?' He turns to me. I nod, then he asks for two. What a wonderful, dependable man. I can't believe how lucky I am to have a man like this as a husband.

I try to take the champagne from the stewardess without taking my eyes off him, but as I reach over a tiny drop of champagne spills from my glass.

'I'm terribly sorry,' the stewardess says, flustered, and she begins wiping his knee with a hand towel.

'It's OK.'

Though he was completely pale just a moment ago, he looks completely calm as he takes the towel and wipes my hand. Maybe it's because he'd seen the stewardess walking around the cabin. Or maybe he just didn't want anyone other than me to see him scared. What a kind person he is.

'I'm sorry,' I say.

'No, no. I'm sorry,' she replies. I freeze when she responds to my apology with a smile.

Right away, I know what she's up to. You have your eyes on my husband, don't you, you bitch? I bet she spilled that champagne on purpose. So she could wipe his knee with the towel. Bet she normally doesn't make so much fuss over just a few drops. Glaring at her back as she walks away, I casually unfold the towel. Good! I thought maybe she might have written her mobile number on it. But I was still worried and it looked as if I wouldn't be able to catch a wink during the twelve-hour flight. She might launch her plot to snare him the moment I let down my guard. You never know where evil lies in this world. There are traps laid everywhere, ready specifically to ruin my immense happiness and plunge me into despair. So I can't relax, no matter where I am. Everybody hates me. And everybody wants him. Where can we go where I won't have to worry? Where can we be safe, where can we think only about each other?

'Promise me we'll be together forever.'

'What are you saying all of a sudden?'

'Does that mean you won't stay with me?'

'Of course I will. I was just wondering why you suddenly said that.'

'I began to feel worried, that's all.'

'You always are. You worry too much.'

'That's not true. It's always justified.'

'All right, all right.' And he holds my hand tight. Not because he's scared, I think. But because I'm so dear to him.

'I'm going to play solitaire now,' I say to him. 'Let's play together.'

'Together? How?'

'How about we team up? I'll operate the control keys and you can be in charge of the select button.'

'I think I'll just watch a movie.'

That was cold of him. But when I pout and tell him so, he pulls the monitor out and uses the control pad to bring solitaire up on the screen.

'I don't know how to work this,' I fuss. So he translates the English control instructions for me. What a wonderful husband. Solitaire and a movie. We're doing different things, but we are affectionate with each other and really enjoying a wonderful flight.

About ten minutes later our meal is served. I was worried that the same Japanese stewardess might come over again, but this time it's a foreign, middle-aged stewardess.

'Meat? Fish?' she asks in broken Japanese.

'One meat, one fish,' he replies, without even asking

me. He's right, though. We always order different things, then share. He knows that whenever we go out to dinner, whatever he's eating always starts to look really good to me, so I always ask for a bite. That's why he always orders different things for us now. We're on the same wavelength and I'm so happy I could die.

'Don't you wish the plane would crash?' I say to him. 'Then we could be together until the very end. Wouldn't that be wonderful?'

'Hey, you! Don't say that! If this plane goes down, it'll be your fault for tempting fate.'

'I hate it when you address me like that. I've told you over and over not to call me "you" like that. How could you even think of calling your wife "you"? I really wish this plane goes down right now. I'm going to pray that it happens. You wait and see! If you don't take it back, I'm going to pray that the plane falls! I'll pray to the gods – put a curse on it! Are you ready for that?'

'All right, I'm sorry.' He says and calls me by my name.

What a horrible guy. Unbelievable. Calling his wife 'you'. Then, as I sit there fuming, I notice that the middle-aged stewardess is still standing there holding the tray with a troubled look on her face.

'Come on, move over,' he says. So I stop leaning on him and shift back properly into my seat. He pulls down my table for me and the woman puts the tray on it, then leaves – all the time wearing a smile on her face. He really is a wonderful husband.

'I'm sorry about what I said. The plane won't crash.

I've got the power to make sure it doesn't. Have faith in me. I promise it won't crash.'

Another foreign stewardess comes over and asks, 'Something to drink?' in bad Japanese. Again, without asking me, he orders red and white wine. I'm just wondering if he could be any more perfect, when suddenly my head starts to fill up with worries again. So when the stewardess takes his glass and pours white wine into it, I seize the opportunity to flip over his coaster. I thought maybe the Japanese stewardess had used one of her colleagues to deliver her phone number to him. But it seems I was wrong.

'What's the matter?' he asks, a puzzled look on his face.

'Nothing,' I say, while checking the coaster on my tray as well – nothing on mine either. I was wondering if maybe she'd anticipated us switching meal trays and so put the number under the coaster on my tray. *Perhaps that stewardess wasn't after him after all? Perhaps she'd simply wiped his knee out of kindness*, I think to myself. Then my eyes catch sight of the napkin around the silverware. I wonder if perhaps her number is on the edge of that.

'Let me get that for you,' I say, picking it up and spreading it out, then laying it on his knees – all the while making sure there's nothing written on it. I sigh with relief, then check my own napkin before spreading it on my lap.

After we finish eating both halves of our meals, we go

back to the movie and solitaire. Unable to finish a game I get bored and kill time by peaking in on the movie he's watching and holding his hand. Then, all of a sudden, that stewardess reappears – coming down the aisle collecting the trays of the people who have finished eating! Well, you'd better not spill anything this time, woman. And holding his hand tightly, I repeat these words in my mind over and over again to put a curse on her. When she reaches us, she takes my tray first. I watch her hand, thinking, *I'll kill you if you dare make even the slightest contact with him. I'll kill you, you hear?*

She takes the tray without any mishaps. Good. She didn't touch him. I feel sleepy with relief. Or maybe I've just had a little too much to eat. I was planning to keep my eye on her for the entire flight to make sure she didn't try anything with him. But now I can feel myself starting to drift off.

'Hey . . .' I call to him.

'Yeah?' he replies with his headphones on and still looking at the screen, but with a face that seemed to ask, 'You say something?'

'I said, hey!'

'What is it?'

'I'm about to fall asleep.'

'Well, wrap up warm then. Aren't you going to wear the socks?'

'I'm fine. The blanket's big.' I kick my legs under the blanket to show him, and he nods 'all right then' and goes back to the screen. I want to kid around with him and say, 'Hey! What's with that uncaring attitude?' But I'm too comfortable with my seat reclined all the way back, so instead I close my eyes and keep hold of his hand.

I open my eyes just a little, but the cabin is dark and for a second I don't know where I am. Oh, right. Honeymoon. Tahiti. Going home to Japan. Seeking asylum. Fake visa. Human organ trafficking . . . I blink a couple of times and catch sight of his back. He's putting on his slippers, maybe in preparation to go to the lavatory. I realise I'm clutching the pillow that was under my head and I put it back there. Then, just as I'm about to reach out for him, he stands up and goes walking down the aisle. I'd wanted to ask him to bring me back something sweet, but oh well. I was about to close my eyes again. Then I realised: I'd been tricked.

There must have been sleeping pills mixed in with my wine. That stewardess must have waited until I'd fallen asleep, then told him to meet her in the lavatory! So that's where he's heading. To meet her!

All is lost. Death is my only option. It's all over. My life is over. I can't imagine life without him. If he cheats on me even once, I will never be able to live happily with him. But at the same time, I don't think I'll be able to divorce him and go to court and all that. So the only path left for me is to go through a living hell, then commit suicide. Even if I survive the living hell, divorce him and try to find hope in another man, after being betrayed by him I'll probably never be able to trust a man again. I'll be unhappy for the rest of my life. I mean, he is the only man I've been able to trust this much in my life. I'd never known true love until I met him. The romances before I met him weren't even romances. They were nothing more than the primitive act of a man and a woman meeting and copulating. It was only when I met him that I was able to experience true human love for the first time. To think that all that happiness is about to be destroyed by just one stewardess!

I pray that the plane will crash. He's probably in the lavatory by now. He may already be touching the stewardess waiting inside. His hands may already be touching her. Those hands of my precious husband. Touching. That woman. I want to die. Just thinking about it gives me goose bumps and my entire body is shaking with rage.

Why should I have to go through this? Why, why, why? It's not fair. I love him so much. I adore him. All I want is to stay with him forever. How can he even think of going with a woman like that? How could you? You just told me you'd never leave me. How could you?!

I wanted to stay with him forever. That's why I broke up with my previous boyfriend. That's why I cut off all contact with past boyfriends and other male friends and focused all my attention on him. I told myself he was the only person in my life. And it was true. He was the only one who could understand my language. Though all my friends, my family, and everyone I work with are Japanese and speak Japanese, I could never communicate with any of them. No matter who I spoke with, we misunderstood each other, resentment built and we would end up quarrelling. Perhaps my linguistic and comprehension skills are inferior. But at any rate, it was impossible for me and someone else to understand each other. I was certain this was the case.

But he was different. He understood exactly what I wanted to say and the more we talked, the more I felt in sync with him. I felt like I had finally met a creature of the same species. A natural treasure thought to be the only one of its kind left in the world, incredibly, amazingly, meeting another of the same kind for the first time. All I could think about was being with him. So naturally we got married and I was ready to give myself wholly to him – body and soul. Sure, I might have annoyed him by saying that I wanted to be with him always, that I couldn't bear to be apart from him for even a moment. But that was proof of my love, proof that I'd never love anyone else, proof that I could only relate to him. I'd never been able to connect with anyone else. Now, finally, I'd found the one person with whom I could. It was only natural then that I would want to be with him all the time. But him? He goes off with that stewardess! Afterwards, he may well come back. But even then, he will have left something with her. That necessary something we needed to love each other.

My eyes are welling up with tears and I think I'm going to start crying. No. No, no, I mustn't. I mustn't cry. I want him to tell me the truth. If he cheated on me, if he really did it, then I want him to tell me honestly. If he sees me crying, he might try to spare my feelings and not tell me the truth. I need to wear a serious look on my face, the look of an adult woman. Then I can just ask him, 'What did you do?' And he might tell me. He knows I hate lies.

If he's honest with me and tells me that he cheated on me, I'll just smile and leave him. I might cry a little. I'll probably feel let down. But I'll be OK. I won't throw a fit. If he tells me he's cheated on me, I won't die. No, actually, I think I might. I think I might actually die. But even so, I shouldn't show my weakness to him. I have to smile and break up with him.

I have to tell him, 'It's OK.'

I have to say, 'I won't blame you.'

I have to tell him, 'I won't get angry at you. I won't cry. So tell me the truth. I'll even go submit the divorce papers on my own. So tell me.' Please, please, whatever you do, don't you do it with the stewardess then come back and lie to me that 'There was a long line for the lavatory'.

I'll tell him, 'I'll be OK. I'll be OK, so don't lie to me.'

I'll say, 'If you did it, if you did it with that stewardess, then just give it to me straight. Tell me that you did it with that stewardess.'

I wonder, has he already kissed her? Just like the first time we kissed. What am I thinking? His kiss with that stewardess couldn't be the same as a kiss between me and him. Oh, what am I supposed to do? He might be lifting her skirt right this moment. He could be thrusting his fingers into her hot flesh. My entire body is sizzling with anger, trembling with it. Just the thought that he might be getting aroused and getting a hard-on for another woman makes me curse and pray that the plane will crash before anything else can happen. *Now, come on! Crash! Come on, crash, crash now!* I pray to myself. But the plane isn't falling from the sky and I stamp my feet in frustration. Why isn't the world programmed so that it will self-destruct the instant he cheats on me? That way I won't have to live in a world in which he's cheated on me. Oh, I want to die, I want to die, I want the world in which he cheated on me to be destroyed!

Now calm down and think straight, I say to myself. A world that self-destructs the moment he cheats on me? Now that doesn't make much sense. *I* should be the one that automatically self-destructs the moment he cheats on me. That way we wouldn't have to inconvenience others. I should install a bomb inside my body and have a remote detonator attached to his dick. But it's too late to be thinking of this stuff. He's probably already doing it with the stewardess anyway. No. Me blowing up isn't enough. I want the whole world to be destroyed.

Has he already put it inside her? I mean, how many seconds have passed since he went to the lavatory? Surely they'd have slipped into the lavatory straight away, all fired up. They'd be all over each other and he'd get it up her immediately. Aaargh! I bet his cock is already rubbing up inside her pussy. I want to die already. I'm doomed. I just want to die now. Can't this plane fall out of the sky? Can't the whole world just come to an end? Can't it even just be the end of me? If only I had nitroglycerin inside me.

I wonder if I can overdose on sleeping pills. Then I remember I haven't brought enough with me for that. Oh this really can't get any worse. There probably aren't any knives on the plane and I don't know where I would be able to hang myself. It's all over, I'm going to die. I'm going to die. Going to kill myself. I can just feel my cells beginning to kill themselves off. Good for me. I hope my cells were made so that they sense the moment he cheats on me. I hope they imagine my pain and despair when I find out about his cheating and die off rather than make me endure the torment. I'll be so glad. I could die a peaceful death. Without ever learning about his cheating. Are they passionately at it with each other right now? He's taking far too long. It must be a minute already since he got up. He should die. Everyone should die. Die, die, die! Let me die.

'You woke up?'

I turn my face and see him there. I feel like crying and I can't speak.

'I thought you might wake up soon, so I brought you a snack.'

He hands me a cookie and an orange juice, then sits down beside me and immediately fastens his seatbelt. Tears well up in my eyes as I bite into the cookie. They trickle down my cheeks as I drink my juice.

'What's the matter?' he asks, looking into my eyes.

I hand him the glass and bury my face in his chest, wiping my tears on his shirt.

'Did you have a scary dream?'

I nod my head again and again, holding on tight to him. Then I feel something warm enveloping my head. His large hand. Just a few moments ago I'd been on the brink of total despair. But now I'm snuggled up against his chest, clinging on tight.

'You're going to spill your juice,' he says.

'I'm so happy I could die.'

'I told you not to say things like that. It's your fault if this plane crashes.'

What a wonderful husband. My adorable husband. I'd die if we ever parted.

I can predict 80 per cent of the conversation I'm about to have. Normally, I have a bad memory, but Shin and I have had this same conversation so many times that I've memorised it. And the fact that we've been discussing the same thing ever since we got married probably means it'll never be resolved. But that's not what I want. So I'm going to talk to him about it. Even though I know it's really just a waste of time. But we can't not have this conversation. I have no intention of not having this conversation.

'Shin, why do you always shut yourself up in your room?'

'I've already told you so many times! I need some time alone.'

'If we're in love, don't you think we should be together?'

'Those are two entirely different matters.'

'But what do you need time alone for?'

'For my mental health. For myself. It's just something I need.'

'What do you do all by yourself? Do you play video games, read books, that kind of thing?'

'It's not a question of what I do with it. I just need that kind of space. Let me ask you, Rin . . . Why do you think it's so important that we're together all the time?'

'We love each other, so we ought to be together as much as possible. We could die tomorrow. I can't bear the thought of not being able to spend the precious time left together.'

'Don't say things like that. If I thought I was going to die tomorrow, I wouldn't even be able to go to work. If I don't have some time alone I can't stay myself. I become unstable and get stressed out. I simply can't live without having some time alone.'

'So you're saying that you'd rather get divorced than give up your time alone?'

'I'm just saying that I wouldn't be able to stay with you if you forced me to be with you all the time.'

'So I should just put up with it?'

'I guess so. But it's only natural. I would be dead if I didn't have any time to myself.'

'What if I told you I'd leave you if we couldn't spend all our time together? Would you leave me?'

'Yes, I suppose I would.'

The desire to be wanted by a man. The desire to get a man. Most females go into hysterics if either of these can't be fulfilled or the fulfilment of these two desires is unbalanced. Their pussies get all irritable, restless. What is hysteria, after all? It's a disease of the pussy.

'My pussy's mad.'

'What? Not your hysteria again.'

'Shut up, you asshole. It's your fault I'm not satisfied, so don't give me that look. That blank look. That condescending look! You're always wearing that face that says women are fools. Why is it that I always want you so bad, but you always, always push me away with a cool expression on your face. Trying to act cool, you bastard? You think you're a cool beauty or something? Go to hell!'

'I'm going to get back to work.'

'In your damn room!'

'Well, you're having one of your hysteria attacks, right?'

'So you think you're going to go just shut yourself up in your room? It's precisely because you hole yourself up in that room that we're having this argument!'

'I can't stand female hysteria,' he says, and leaves the room.

'You bastard!' I shout after him. 'Do you want to die? I'll break down that door of yours with an axe and make my own version of *The Shining*!'

My words bounce off his back as he closes the door to his room. I put on the earphones of my portable CD player and listen to *Non-stop Trance Adventure*. As I dance,

I begin to feel warm and turn off the heat. I wonder why I'm such a difficult person and I look up at the heater and think of my stubbornness. Tears stream down my face, but I keep on dancing.

'So sorry to make you come all this way. Please, over here. What would you like to drink Miss Takahara? And you'll be smoking, won't you? I'll get you an ashtray if you could just wait for a moment.'

Kobayashi blurts all this out in one breath before standing up.

The hotel looks exactly the same as when I came here a week earlier for an interview – standing still in the middle of the city looking all sad and disappointed. Looking up at it made me dizzy. I know all I have to do is not look up, but I can't help myself. So every time I come here I get dizzy.

Kobayashi returns with an ashtray from a nearby table, then drops down onto the sofa opposite me. There weren't any non-smoking seats in this lobby, so all the tables should really have an ashtray and matches on them anyway. I wonder why just this table didn't have an ashtray and look at Kobayashi. It had to be a ploy of his because he'd recently been trying to stop smoking, because he gets all fidgety every time I light a cigarette. How annoying he is.

'Please, please, go ahead,' he says. 'The interview is from five, so please relax for a while. What would you like to drink?'

'A café latte. With extra whipped cream.' I catch his expression cloud over slightly the second I say that.

'I'll go order, then,' he says, getting to his feet again.

I notice that his smile is a little twisted. I'm always observing. So I notice things like that. You know, if I watch someone for long enough I can even get a pretty good idea of when they're going to die. No, that's a lie. No, actually it's true. But as long as I just think that and never tell anyone, then it's neither a lie nor the truth.

I'm always entertaining silly thoughts like these, so my mind is always ringing with the sound of me talking to myself. I live with the sole purpose of making my boring life even more boring by providing a boring commentary for my boring everyday life through a boring voice in my head. Sometimes I feel like there are several people living inside me. But that's not the case. It's a delusion. Because everything inside me is me. There are several billion selves inside me. And there's the 'me' that serves as a wrapping, holding them all together. All those billions coming together to make one 'me'. Since there are several billion living inside me, there are so many contradictions in the things I say and think. But they are just contradictions caused by the many selves inside my wrapping. It wouldn't be so bad if I could just think of it that way. But in the end, I was the one that had to take responsibility for all these contradictions.

Whenever I get stuck in a difficult situation, I wish I could call on an inner self that just happens to be living in a faraway country, then get that self to take over. But it's precisely at times like this that all those inners selves gang up on me and make me take full responsibility. I laugh under my breath and light a cigarette, feeling the thoughts of all my selves beginning to fragment once more.

'Is something the matter?' Kobayashi asks with a puzzled look, having just returned to his seat. He wants to know why I'm smiling. I need to stay calm. Remember I'm not being interrogated. Remember not to behave like a victim. Shin told me it's not good to play the victim all the time.

'Oh. Nothing. So what's the interview about today?'

'Come on now, Miss Takahara. You've looked at the outline I gave you, haven't you?'

'Sorry. I glanced through it, but there were so many different sheets I couldn't tell which one I was supposed to read.'

'I thought that might be the case, so I printed one out for you before coming. Here you go.'

I flip through the sheets of paper, but I can't register the words in my brain. Perhaps because there's almost no indentation, they just look like big blocks of text. Several square blocks of words fly into my mind as diagrams. I guess you could call it word-blindness – I get it quite a lot these days. Even when I'm looking over a manuscript I've written, the words on the page start to look like nothing more than diagrams and I can't under-stand what they say.

When did I first start having these symptoms . . . ? Actually, who cares when it started? I don't care if I've had it since birth. After I successfully convince myself of this, I take a scoop of whipped cream from my latte. *I'd better at least read the title of the outline,* I tell myself, and I look at the top of the page. I see the words 'Dreamer's Dream.' I've been doing a lot of interviews for Kobayashi, who is eager to promote my book, which came out last month, but I'm rapidly getting tired of interviewers who refuse to recognise the difference between me and the character in my novel. That's why I've mistakenly decided on a whim that I will try something a little 'different', shall we say. I mean, come on, I don't think anyone would call me a dreamer.

'Well, it's basically about dreams,' says Kobayashi.

'Yes, I see.'

But did it mean dream as in 'future, aspirations and dreams' or as in 'I dreamt last night that I was walking along a narrow road in the distant north, when suddenly I came across a Darth Vader mask'? That's right, Darth Vader. That's the dream I had last night. But I suppose Darth Vader isn't really fashion magazine material.

'So you really think they expect me to have anything to say about hopes, aspirations and dreams?'

Kobayashi looks a little surprised, then glances down at the sheet under my hand from the other side of the table.

'Well, of course not,' he says. 'It's about the kind of dreams you have at night. It says so right here, "Ask the author about her recent dreams."'

Oh, right, I think to myself and I try, unsuccessfully,

to find the part he's talking about. But, it has to be written somewhere, so I nod anyway. *What should I do?* I think. If I don't think of something quick, I'll end up talking about the Darth Vader episode, because it's the only dream I can remember right now and there's no way it'd be acceptable to share a dream as boring as that. I have to say something more humorous. Some short funny episode. Something clever. I have to make up some interesting story. Then, as I sit there trying to think what to say while pretending to listen to Kobayashi, the interview crew arrives and I end up talking for an hour about my stupid Darth Vader mask dream and in doing so revealing something about my mental health that I shouldn't – that I am wrought with frustration.

What a blunder. What a stupid woman I am. Stupid, stupid, stupid. The interview crew packs up and goes home and Kobayashi hands me another bunch of print-outs.

'What's this?' I ask him.

'The outline for the second interview.'

I take the sheets from him and freeze for a second. *Hey Kobayashi! It was supposed to be just one, not two. Trying to trick me, aren't you?* I think to myself. Then I glance at the sheet and the layout looks familiar. So it's my mistake after all. I need to stay calm. Restrain myself. I have this tendency to always think I'm right and make others feel bad. I need to remember that even I'm wrong sometimes. That even I fail sometimes. That I need to be more tolerant towards myself and towards others. Shin always says, 'Rin, you consider other people to be less than human.' What a horrible guy he is. It's been two years since we started going out, we've been married a year, and he still continues to misunderstand me. I think it's because he has no interest in me and doesn't pay serious attention to me – that's why he misunderstands me. If he really understood me, he'd never think I looked down on people. I open myself completely to others and I live my life ready to accept anything and everything. Oh. I need to stop right there. I think my pussy is about to have a tantrum again.

Women who become paranoid that they aren't loved have a tendency to go into hysterics. In other words, they have a tendency to be like I am now. But because I can see that, it shows how understanding I am. Surely there can't be even ten women in this world with my level of objectivity. I feel that I might be beginning to contradict myself now, so I stop myself and let out a little snort. Kobayashi catches it, though, and makes a disgusted face. What do people think when they know they've been snorted at? That they're being ridiculed, maybe. That must make them feel pretty lousy.

'I'm sorry,' I offer.

'Huh, about what?'

'I was being a little arrogant.'

'What? Why?'

'Oh. Never mind.'

I wonder how someone might feel when somebody who has just snorted at them suddenly apologises.

'It's just . . . Never mind. It's fine.'

'Huh? Sorry, what is?'

I'm just about to tell him that it's nothing really, when I suddenly realise that would only sound suspicious. Surely it'd be better to make up a false reason to apologise rather than to retract the apology I'd made without offering a reason.

'I just remembered how cute that pen was,' I said. 'The one the previous interviewer had.'

'Oh, was it?'

How did we get talking about this anyway? I think about it and remember. Right, this conversation started with me snorting. But if that was the case, then surely there was a fault in my logic. After all, why would I have snorted when thinking about the interviewer's cute pen? If I'd really been thinking about the cute pen, I would've probably smiled and tilted my head with a kind, ladylike expression, wondering to myself where I could buy one just like it. I needed to make up another excuse, show him that I was sane. Oh, what a bother it was, having to talk to people!

'No, no. That's not what I meant. Um, it's like, yeah, that interviewer, he had an unbelievable face.'

'I was thinking the same thing. It was some face.'

'Wasn't it? I almost laughed when I saw him. I'm sorry, it's just that I thought I shouldn't really say that someone had a strange face, so I made up some silly excuse about a pen.'

'When I saw you smiling, I guessed that you were probably

23

thinking about that guy's face. It was an incredible face, really.'

'Yeah, really, it was incredible.'

Phew. That worked. Finally it's all worked out. Everything is OK now. There is no need for me to worry anymore. What a relief. I take a sip of my latte and meditate for a while. This is a skill I've learned recently – the ability to meditate while making small talk with someone.

So I'm sitting here thinking things that aren't even true. No, actually, that are true. As if it matters anyway. I must be stupid to be thinking the things I'm thinking. Anyway, then the next interview crew arrives. Oh, and I've forgotten to read the outline again. I receive business cards from the interviewer, editor and cameraman. All three of them are women. In fact, they're sipping-herb-tea-out-on-an-open-terrace, scented-candles-in-bath, 'lose-six-pounds-by-summer'-written-in-their-diary kind of women. I sit up in my seat and glance at the outline, only to see the title, *Independent Woman*, which literally makes me feel sick. Why did I agree to such an interview? Did I really even say that I would take it? Could this be one of Kobayashi's conspiracies after all? Kobayashi seems to place a high priority on interviews with women's magazines. In his ignorance he probably assumed, '*Independent Woman*! This will be good publicity for the book . . .' and then agreed to it without consulting me.

'Thank you so much for agreeing to this interview.'

'And thank you for taking the time.'

I'm alternating between glaring at Kobayashi suspiciously and glancing through the outline, when suddenly it all comes back to me. Shin had noticed this outline arrive on our fax machine at home and had said teasingly, 'Wonder why they're asking you of all people, Rin, to do an interview on the theme *Independent Woman*?' That made me get all defensive and that's why I'd insisted on taking the interview. What a stupid woman I am. If only the theme were *Stupid Woman*. Then I'd have plenty to say.

Of course, if I wanted to, I could just shrug my shoulders and say, 'Oh well, it's their fault for asking me to do an interview on independent women.' But I've agreed to do it and so I feel I have to say something an independent woman would say. So while the cameraman is setting up the lighting, I prepare my independent woman face. I'm almighty. I can do anything. I'm the ultimate independent woman.

'Right then, first can you tell us what kind of person you think is an independent woman?'

'Well, one thing I can say for sure is that it isn't someone like me.'

Why did I give such a dead-honest response after going to all that trouble putting on my independent woman face? I mean, the fact that this woman has requested an interview with me for an article on 'independent women' must mean that she thinks I'm one of them. What is she thinking now that I've contradicted her with my very first answer? She has to be wondering why I agreed to do this interview.

'But Miss Takahara, you're wedded and you have a career. And I read in another magazine interview that you do housework as well. To be able to balance your family and work life like that suggests that you are independent. Are you saying that you personally experience feelings of not being independent?' The interviewer has an affected way of speaking, putting an annoying emphasis on the words 'wedded', 'you personally' and 'experience feelings'.

I don't want to confuse her image of 'wedded' life with my marriage. That's an unpleasant thought. Although, to be honest, I've had a bad feeling ever since I saw this interviewer's face. The instant I saw her, I knew. If I weren't an author, this woman would be looking down on me at this very moment. She'd be wondering what is wrong with this vulgar woman in front of her. But instead, here she is using overly polite language and smiling at me just because I'm the subject of her interview. And using that word, 'wedded'! What was she thinking? Just say 'married'! Then suddenly, I remember my bad habit of imitating the way people speak when they're bothering me and I feel faint. So I tell myself that all I have to do is have them send me the draft later and I can revise it.

'It is true that I am able to balance my family and work life. But my work can be done at home. Therefore, I would say that it's more like a daily chore than a job. So it's really nothing particularly worthy of mention.'

What a grotesquely pompous manner I'm speaking in. Kobayashi notices my strange tone and looks up from his planner at me. I need to fix this. What's more, it isn't very literary. I'll be laughed at for speaking like this when my job is all about working with words.

I'm forming impressions in my mind about her every word and my every word, and before I know it, it's been almost an hour and the interview is over. I don't like talking to people. When I talk to people, all the things about myself that I don't like come to the surface. I don't like knowing about myself. It's tantamount to torture to have to understand, acknowledge and accept each and every one of my several hundred million selves. It's self-derision, a one-player game, a one-person performance.

'That went very well. Here you go.'

I stare at the sheet that Kobayashi is holding out and cock my head.

'Is this . . . ?' I moan and Kobayashi responds with a surprised look. It's the outline for a third interview. Surely something is wrong here? I don't remember agreeing to this. This time it really has to be a conspiracy by Kobayashi. But wait. Before I start suspecting others, I should suspect the many selves inside me.

'I'm just going to the bathroom.'

'Right. Please go ahead. In the meantime, can I get you something else to drink?'

'Whipped cream.'

'Just whipped cream?'

'Yes.'

Kobayashi's face looks slightly annoyed again. It doesn't bother me when he makes a face. If it did, I wouldn't say these things. I only say these kinds of things to people who will either gladly fulfil my request or who I couldn't care less if they make a face. So convenient of me to make these rules.

I walk into the bathroom where the lights are so bright they give me a headache and I immediately call Shin.

'Hello? What's the matter?'

'I want to ask you something. Did I mention to you that I was going to be doing an interview for a feature called 'I Believe in UFOs' in *UFO Communication* magazine'?

'Yeah you did. I tried to stop you.'

'And what did I say my intention in doing the interview was?'

'You read the interview outline when we were out drinking at a bar the other day. You were drunk and said *This is hilarious* and insisted that you were going to take it. You called Mr Kobayashi there and then to tell him you would. So I suppose that it wasn't really a question of intention. You just took it because it sounded fun. Don't you remember any of this?'

'I remember now. Thanks.'

I hang up and stare at the mirror. Tears well up in my eyes. Why does this always happen? There is never, ever any consistency in my actions. And everything always ends up a disaster. Unable to take it, I give Shin another call and he answers straight away.

'What's the matter?' He says, clearly annoyed.

'I can't do this, I want to go home. Shin, come and sit

through the interview with me. Not only do I not believe in UFOs, but I only think about them perhaps once every two years. I can't possibly give a proper interview. Shin, please, you have to come!'

'That's impossible.'

'Why?'

'It's just not possible. I have two meetings.'

'What's more important? Your meetings or poor me who has to talk about UFOs?'

'My meetings! It's your fault for taking it when you were drunk.'

'What good's that going to do, bringing that up now? The interview crew will be here in about ten minutes.'

'So figure something out yourself.'

'You're heartless.'

'Listen, I have to go to my meeting now.'

'Hey, why are you acting all distant?'

'If you'll please excuse me.'

'Hey! Why are you acting like a stranger?'

I get disconnected. Left with no choice, I begin to think about UFOs. UFOs exist. They definitely do. They come from around the Pluto area. I'm sure they do . . . I try to picture UFOs and aliens in detail. UFOs most definitely exist. This world is full of things that can't be explained by science. I believe in the mysteries of the universe. No, actually, I've seen a UFO. That's right. When I was a child I once saw a glowing golden doughnut-shaped UFO. That's right. I'd just forgotten about it. I've seen a UFO. And in detail too . . . Why, why in such detail? That's right. When

I was a child I was abducted by a UFO. I just hadn't been able to remember it for the longest time, because the aliens had erased my memory. That's right, I've been abducted by a UFO . . .

'I can't do it,' I moan and go back to the lobby. I ignore Kobayashi, who isn't looking too well, and sit down on the sofa.

'Hey! Whipped cream! It looks delicious,' I say.

Kobayashi's expression seems to lighten up a little on seeing me eat the glassful of whipped cream. It's human nature to feel good when your efforts pay off. Even if something is hard or unpleasant, when those efforts pay off all is forgotten. I had risked the danger of being thought of as a selfish woman, so that he could experience this happiness. You should be grateful Kobayashi!

While these thoughts are going through my head, the interview crew arrives. There's no writer and it appears that the macho guy who introduced himself as the editor of *UFO Communication* is going to be doing the interviewing. He sits down across from me. Hey, I should first ask him why he thought about interviewing *me* on this topic. I'll make a pre-emptive strike and get ahead while I can, I think. And just as I open my mouth, the guy begins to talk – forcing me to shut it.

'Thank you very much for agreeing to this interview. I requested the interview on the off chance that you might be interested, so I was pleasantly surprised when you agreed to it.'

'Um, well, um, thank you.'

'All your novels have such a mystical quality to them. It got me wondering where this quality came from. And I thought that perhaps you believed in paranormal phenomena – ghosts, UFOs, that kind of thing.'

My novels? Mystical? What a nice thing to say. It is true that my novels generally have a mystical quality to them. Anything without a mystical quality to it doesn't interest me. But to connect that with paranormal phenomena like ghosts and UFOs seems such a simplistic interpretation. Does this guy think I'm dependent on the existence of UFOs? Man, it pisses me off. It makes me so angry. But I don't go into hysterics in these kinds of situations. I have promised Shin that I won't lose my cool in public.

'First of all, can you tell me what made you begin to believe in UFOs?'

'Actually, I don't think UFOs exist.'

The interviewer, cameraman and Kobayashi all freeze. Now I have to do something about their frustration, their feelings of being duped and the displeasure they're feeling this instant. I need to make an excuse. One that will satisfy them. But this is going to be a major undertaking. Am I up to it? That's right. This is where my legend as a great woman is going to begin . . .

'I have to say you really did catch me by surprise. Saying that you don't believe in UFOs for an article entitled 'I Believe in UFOs' for a magazine about UFOs. I was even a little moved.'

Kobayashi's words don't touch me at all. Moved? How can he say that when I was embarrassed enough to want to take the chopsticks in front of me and stab myself in the throat? Could he possibly be any more clueless? Then again, perhaps Kobayashi is aware of my embarrassment and is just saying that to alleviate it. If so, I should be grateful to him for his kindness. And I should admonish myself for thinking he's clueless. But wait. What if Kobayashi is aware of how embarrassed I am and said what he did to make me feel even more embarrassed? If that's the case, I'm the one who is clueless for thinking he's clueless. And I should feel hatred towards him for ridiculing me like that. I respect people who love me, but hate people who disrespect me.

'So, how is it going? The manuscript.'

'Manuscript?'

'Yes. How's it coming along?'

The manuscript . . . coming along. That's a whole different matter.

'It's coming along.'

There are always times when you have to lie.

'Is that right? I'm really glad to hear that. Do you think you'll make the deadline?'

The manuscript coming along and the deadline are two entirely different matters. Just because it's coming along, it doesn't mean I'm going to meet the deadline. If it really were coming non-stop, then I wouldn't be eating with Kobayashi like this. I'd be sitting in front of my computer at home right this moment. This isn't an excuse.

'Sure, I'll be certain to finish it by then.'

And there are times when you have to pile one lie on top of another.

'Are you sure? If there is anything I can help you with, please don't hesitate to ask. I was a little worried because I kind of pushed this series on you immediately after your new book came out. But our editorial department is really excited. They're looking forward to seeing what kind of manuscript you prepare for the first instalment.'

So you're pressuring me now, huh? Who do you think you are, Kobayashi?

'It's been a while since I wrote a long piece so I'm looking forward to it, too.'

'Huh . . . ?'

'No, I mean I'm enjoying writing it.'

Kobayashi appears a little suspicious for a second, but immediately picks up one of the small dishes as if he'd thought better of it. Eating with this guy always gets me down. No, that isn't it. I'm always feeling down, except when I'm with Shin. That's why I always want to be with him. That's why it's so hard when he shuts himself up in his room. When the fact that he doesn't want to be with me is expressed in his actions, I feel unending despair in every second. Despair by the second. Each day this is surely and gradually eating away at my soul.

When I get home I say *I'm home!* to Smith-Smith. I know Shin isn't home. After dinner, I'd had a couple of drinks at the bar, then said goodbye to Kobayashi, got in a taxi and called Shin straight away. But I got the answerphone. They probably all went drinking after their meeting.

I call out to Smith-Smith, who has to be somewhere in the room. There is no response. I don't think much of it, but, still feeling down, I head over to the desk in the corner of the living room. I need to write that manuscript for Kobayashi. The sound of the computer starting up reverberates through the quiet room and I still don't understand why I accepted Kobayashi's request. A different self from the one that writes, a self that surfaced when I was drunk, must have said "'Sure, I can write it,'" because it certainly had nothing to do with me. It's strange that I, the writer, have to take responsibility for a job that a different self agreed to. But if I say that I can't take the job because the self that took the job was a different person, people would only think I'd lost my mind. I haven't lost my mind. I could even say my sole reason for living is to prove that fact. But if someone affirmed my sanity by simply saying the words 'You are sane', then I'm sure I'd remain unconvinced. I go on proving my sanity every day by writing fiction, talking to people or making public appearances. But I don't want anyone to endorse my sanity by simply saying, 'You are normal, you are sane.' What a contradiction. But then, the things I think and say are always full of contradictions. I imagine most people are that way. But that doesn't mean I've given up and that I'm living life thinking, *Who cares if I'm contradicting myself*? It's because I'm both dissatisfied and anxious about these contradictions that I languish over these thoughts and lead a life that's not all that different from death.

Shin is the only person who can shine light on such an idle life. Through meeting Shin, I was able to slowly find meaning in my existence. But ever since we started living together he's shut himself away in his room almost every day and keeps causing me to lose sight of the meaning of my life. Why does he push me away? Why does he isolate himself from the country that is me? Why doesn't he live in the world that is me? I just can't understand it. I look up in response to the sound of a tongue clicking, but the room looks the same. It must have been Smith-Smith welcoming me home.

'I'm home,' I say again, but there's no response. What a capricious creature. Smith-Smith doesn't have the communication skills to play catch with words, to answer in response to something I say. It's the same when no matter how many times I throw a ball for him, throw a ball for him, throw a ball for him, Shin will just dodge, dodge, dodge it, and shut himself up in his room. Why doesn't he try to catch the ball? It's a real mystery to me. No, it's no mystery. I'm just trying not to see the answer. But I do actually know why. Shin doesn't have the ability to catch what I throw at him. Or it's that he doesn't have any intention of catching it. It's as simple as that. And I don't have the strength to accept the loneliness of not having my throw caught by my man, so I ignore it and pretend to be puzzled as to why he doesn't try to catch it. It's ridiculous. It doesn't really matter anyway . . . I've been telling myself that something doesn't matter when it really does, and as a result I've gradually turned into an unbalanced woman. I mean, just think about it. I'm blessed with a body that any woman would be happy with. I'm brimming with talent and I've got a beautiful face that's made to be loved. But despite the fact that I have all these things, my body is always wrapped in a foreign object called clothes, my prose packed with my supernatural talent is understood by no one, and my face is always masked in poorly applied make-up. I'm not impressed by the suggestion that I should just stop wearing clothes or make-up. Even if I did stop wearing them, nobody could possibly understand my brilliance. And in the end, brilliance that isn't understood by anyone isn't brilliance anyway. So in other words, is it the case that I'm not brilliant? Now that is an entirely different matter. Basically, anything I don't want to admit to is an entirely different matter.

I sing the tune to *Boléro* in a loud voice. Then, the moment I sit down at my desk and place my fingers on the keyboard they freeze. It's simply that I can't move my fingers and not that I can't write. If my fingers moved properly I could give life to brilliant prose. But my fingertips aren't budging. So it can't be helped. My fingers are probably suffering from rheumatism, but I haven't had the time to go to a hospital for a while now. My everyday life is just full of these failures.

I hear a sound and stop singing. It's the sound of a key in the lock. I jump out of my seat and run to the door. Shin is taking his shoes off when I fling my arms around him and he must have lost his balance as he totters and says, 'Please, later.'

'Nice to have you home, Shin. I had a tough day. I had to talk for an hour about UFOs.'

'So how did it go? Were you able to say what you wanted to?'

'Not at all. It couldn't have gone worse. But Mr Kobayashi praised me.'

'Really? Well, just be sure to read the outlines from now on, OK? And don't accept interviews when you're drunk.'

I tell Shin just how hard my day has been and he strokes my head for me. I ask for a hug and he holds me tight. I'm so, so happy. I'm moved by how warm it feels to hold and be held by someone. I'm moved every day when Shin comes home from work and holds me. When I'm not being held by Shin, I always forget how wonderful it feels.

'How about you, Shin? What did you do today?'

'I had three last-minute meetings scheduled, so it was a busy day.'

'So my puppy worked hard, too, then?'

'I'm not a dog.'

'I know. I'm *your* dog.'

'I want a dog that's more amenable and obedient.'

'How can you ask for more after all I've given you?'

'More amenable and obedient. That's what I want.'

'There's no point asking for more. I can't love you any more than I already do.'

'More than love, I want amenability and obedience.'

'How can you say that?'

'If you love someone, it's normal to try and do what that person wants.'

'But Shin you wanted me the way I was.'

'You used to be amenable and obedient.'

'What's that supposed to mean? Are you saying that I've become selfish?'

'You were amenable. Very.'

'. . . I still am . . .'

If I don't back down here, Shin will immediately shut himself away in his room. He always escapes when someone accuses him or gets angry with him. He's extremely afraid of being accused or scolded. He's like a cowardly dog. But you could say the same about me. I'm afraid that Shin will shut himself up in his room. I'm unable to say what I want to him. I'm a cowardly dog. We're two scared dogs that continue to live together nervously and naively. It's hard living each day like you have something fragile in your hand. But as long as that fragile thing is precious to me, I will go on living nervously and naively. I can't imagine life without Shin. The words 'nervous dogs' come to mind and I write it on the back of my hand with a marker pen. I consider using it as the title for my new series, but immediately change my mind, deciding it's a cliché, and I rub it off.

'What's that?'

'Nothing.'

Shin peers into my face looking perplexed, but unable

to read my expression. He quickly loses interest and turns on the TV. Then after spending about an hour in the living room, he puts his pack of cigarettes in his pocket and stands up saying, 'I'm going to go do some work.'

I try to put on a brave face by sarcastically saying, 'Yeah, I'm sure its real work.' But I end up flinging my arms around his back as he's about to leave the room.

'I won't be long.'

'How long is not long?'

'Not long.'

Shin wraps his warm hands around the hand I extend towards him, then immediately lets go and leaves the room. I hear the door to his room close and I quickly plug the earphones of my portable CD player into my ears. During the few seconds it takes for me to push the play button and for the music to start, a maddening feeling of frustration envelops my entire body. But once *Non-stop Reggae Adventure* starts playing I relax. I know. I'm aware that I'm terrified of the sound of the trunk. The sound of the trunk drives me crazy.

I wonder when I first started hearing the sound of the trunk? It must have been more than six months ago. I can't say for certain, since I've been both consciously and subconsciously trying not to think about the sound of the trunk opening and shutting. Inside the trunk lies Shin's secret. Shin's secret is always sitting inside that trunk. I can't remember when I first became aware of the sound of the trunk, but I do remember very clearly the incident that turned the trunk into an object of fear. Back then I didn't pay much attention to the sound of the trunk opening and shutting every so often when Shin went into his room. *I wonder what it is?* I might have thought in the corner of my mind, but I didn't give it serious thought. Not until then. Not until that incident.

Shin was holed up in his room as usual, so I knocked on his door saying, 'Let's go and eat!' in an attempt to get him out. But Shin said he was almost at the end of his book, so he asked me to wait until he was finished. So I sat down next to his chair and passed the time flipping through some of the difficult books on his shelf. Every now and then the boredom of waiting made me interrupt him, but for the most part I sat silently and obediently on the floor.

Suddenly I got the feeling that something wasn't quite right. It was the trunk – it had been moved slightly from its usual spot in the corner of the room. There's something so unsettling about your furniture being moved. So, almost instinctively, I tried to nudge the trunk back into place with my foot. But the moment I touched it, Shin sprang from his chair and threw his arms around me.

'What? What's up?' I asked him.

But he just pulled me to my feet and said, 'I'm done now, so let's go eat!'

'Is there something in that trunk that you don't want me to see?' I asked him and I saw his face go pale before my eyes. It was the first time I had ever seen him get flustered like that, which made me feel a sense of anguish building inside.

'What? What? What are you getting all flustered for?' I knew he just wanted to get me out of there as soon as possible, but I couldn't stop myself from asking him. But instead of replying, he just scooped me up in his arms and carried me over to the living room.

'What are you doing? I'm not your pet dog, you know. You can't just pick me up and plop me down wherever you want me!'

'Oh come on,' he said in a sickly sweet voice, 'let's just get something to eat. You're hungry, aren't you?'

'Don't try to change the subject. Lately I hear you opening and closing that trunk all the time. Are you hiding something from me in there? And why are you getting all flustered like that? Why?'

But Shin insisted that there was nothing going on, and in the end he left me crying hysterically and went back to his room. Then I heard him open the trunk, close it again, and I heard him close the closet doors, too. So whatever it was he had been hiding, he'd moved it from the trunk to the closet. I shivered at the thought of him keeping secrets from me, no matter what they might be. And as I sat there thinking about it I was overcome by despair so great that I thought I might die.

I never set foot in Shin's room again after that incident. And though it's considered normal practice for a wife to clean her husband's room, I never have and it's likely that I never will. Sometime later I began to hear the familiar sound of the trunk opening and closing again, so I assumed he'd moved his secret back from the closet.

This was no surprise as I knew the trunk had a lock, but from the moment I realised he was keeping a secret from me I felt a sense of growing resentment towards him. How can I possibly trust someone 100 per cent when they hide things or keep secrets from me? And when I want so much to believe him, too. But I don't have the courage to tell him that I want to leave him. And gradually, I adapt to life with his secret – even though the thought of it makes me flustered, makes me unstable, and makes me shudder.

From then, I knew I should never mention the sound of the trunk. And I knew I should never enter Shin's room. I make a point of playing my portable CD player and jamming the earphones into my ears every time he goes into his room – just to make sure that I never hear what he's doing. I also invented a new distraction in the form of Smith-Smith.

I wonder to myself when I first felt the presence of Smith-Smith. But actually, he's a product of my imagination. There is no Smith-Smith in this house. But I live my life with the illusion that there is. Not long after we moved into this apartment – which we started renting just after we got married – I was lying in bed one night, unable to sleep because of a scary story that Shin had told me. I had to go to the bathroom at four in the morning, and right when I flushed the toilet I heard a strange crackling sound that made me jump out of my skin. I rushed back to the bedroom, shook Shin awake, and babbled on that I'd heard a strange noise. But he just brushed it aside, saying it was probably just something that lives here.

'What? What lives here? I can't share a place with some strange creature!'

'Well, it's probably a ghost.'

'A ghost?'

'Yeah. A boy.'

'What kind of boy?'

'Smith.'

'Mr Smith?'

'A white boy with a skinhead.'

'Smith?'

'You can think of a first name for him, Rin.'

'Well, then . . . how about Smith?'

'Smith Smith?'

'Yeah. Sounds impressive, doesn't it?'

'It does. Well let's just try to get along together – all three of us.'

So that was the conversation with a semi-conscious Shin that brought Smith-Smith into existence. But I'd forgotten all about it until the incident with the trunk. I decided that whenever I heard the sound of the trunk from now on, I'd attribute the noise to Smith-Smith playing some sort of prank. And whenever I heard a crack as the building shifted slightly under its own weight or when I heard a sharp noise from the air-conditioning, then I'd attribute them to Smith-Smith just the same. I knew it was a stupid thing to think of and that really there was no Smith-Smith in the house. But I also knew that if I didn't think of Smith-Smith playing his pranks, then I wouldn't be able to go on living. So I made myself believe in Smith-Smith with all my body and soul. I made my life run according to such uncommon rules and conditions. And as a result, I felt I was always at death's door. So close to death that I wanted to die.

The rhythms of *Non-stop Reggae Adventure* reverberate against my eardrums. Now I only listen to non-stop music to make sure I don't make the stupid mistake of catching the sound of the trunk opening or closing in the interval between songs. A stupid mistake? Actually, it's more a case of me being pathetic, pretending that it's rational to buy all these non-stop albums when I've actually bought them out of fear for my own life. I smile to myself, then start playing *Non-stop Techno Adventure* on the main stereo. This way, I can be sure not to hear the sound of the trunk if I come to the end of the CD in my portable player or if it runs out of batteries. And though this may sound excessive, I am actually getting a lot better – I used to have the TV, the stereo, the radio and my portable player on at the same time. There was no way I could just pass the time in silence. But there was no way I could get by with just the music from either the stereo or the portable player alone. If I had any less sound than I do right now, I'd go crazy.

I'm actually proud of myself for having been able to relax as much as I have. But this too is just a foolish illusion. I turn everything into a foolish illusion. So even if all the CDs were suddenly to break and if I were to overhear the sound of the trunk, then I'd just attribute the noise to Smith-Smith, so I could keep telling myself that Shin didn't have a secret. Because if I ever really admitted that he did have a secret, then I would die. I'm such a weak creature like that. Weaker than a dog. Weaker than a rabbit, a turtle, a squirrel, a hamster or a goldfish.

I couldn't get much writing done while listening to *Non-stop Reggae Adventure*. It wasn't as if I'd been making much progress with it in the first place, but listening to *Non-stop Reggae Adventure* made me even less productive. At this rate, there is no way I'm going to make the deadline. In fact, I wonder if I'll even be able to make it in time for the publication date! So I'm just hoping and praying that Kobayashi has given me a date that's a few days earlier than the real deadline. I begin to consider telling them to find someone else for the job. But the possibility of divine inspiration hitting me like a flash and making me jot down thirty pages in one sitting stops me from doing that. I always endure these deadlines in silence, frittering time away until almost the end. Then at the last moment I produce the worst possible results. That's just the way I am. And even though I know this is the way I am, I can't do anything to fix it.

A Spanish restaurant. I mouth these words to myself and suddenly they begin to feel real, like the restaurant in front of me really is Spanish. But is this the restaurant I'm looking for? Or is it the other one? A minute has already passed since I came to a standstill in front of these two adjacent restaurants, and as neither had a menu posted outside and I'd forgotten the name of the place anyway, all I had to go on was my intuition. I should just call Shinagawa. This thought comes to me only after I have asked at the counter if there's a reservation under the name "Shinagawa". The waiter tells me, 'This way please. Your friend is already here.'

I'm relieved to hear this and head over to my seat. I've basically been forced to guess whether Shinagawa would have gone for the restaurant that looked like a posh hangout for the bourgeoisie or the one that looked modern. I'm correct in guessing the latter, and the beige and gold interior is already making me dizzy.

'Hello.'

'Ah, long time no see!' Shinagawa stands up with a friendly smile and remains that way until I'm seated – reminding me of a dog. Unlike me, he exudes good manners. He's wearing a nicely tailored suit. He is also wearing a tie, which is a little unusual for an editor. I recall how Kobayashi had been dressed in jeans the other day and I find the difference dizzying. I wish I didn't, and that dizziness didn't play such a recurring role in my life.

My impression that Shinagawa's suit is well-tailored, however, is completely unfounded. I have no knowledge with which to judge whether or not a suit is well-tailored. I've never had any training that might qualify me to tell the difference, so there's no way I can really tell. But I do think his tie is a nice colour. And by a nice colour I don't just mean an interesting colour.

'What would you like to drink?' he asks.

And off the top of my head I say, 'Something fizzy, like champagne or a champagne cocktail.'

Shinagawa gives me a bemused smile, then orders some champagne, the name of which I'd heard before.

'It really has been a while. Since that party maybe.'

'It has been. You look . . . younger,' I say.

I had been about to say that he looked like he'd matured, but even though I meant it in a purely positive way, I knew that it would only make him feel bad. So instead I thought of saying that he looked tired, but I thought he might take that as a criticism, as if to say, 'How dare you look tired for your meeting with me?!'

So, as a last resort, I end up telling him he looks younger, when what I really wanted to say was that he'd aged in a good way – as if to imply that he gave the impression of being mature and calm. But I just can't communicate my thoughts and feelings the way I want to. So no matter how fond I am of a person, they always end up misunderstanding me at some point. I briefly wonder if I might be better able to communicate my thoughts in writing. But when I consider the fact that my novels are also commonly misunderstood, I decide to abandon any such notion.

'Oh! Do you think so? How about you? Your face seems somehow more relaxed than before. Have you changed your make-up?'

'Oh, you noticed!' I say, smiling, though I know I haven't changed a thing about my make-up since I last saw him. But if I told him that, I'm sure he'd have felt disappointed or felt the need to come up with something else to back up his observation, and I don't like to cause others trouble. Of course, there's a chance he wouldn't have felt troubled at all if I'd told him I hadn't changed my make-up. But that isn't what matters. At least not to me.

The champagne arrives and we drink a toast. Shinagawa takes off his jacket and drapes it over the back of the chair next to him. I notice a ballpoint pen in the inside breast pocket and think of how it might be making a stain on the fabric inside if the nib is out. But that's something I will probably never find out.

'I read the short story about the flight. It was wonderful. But wasn't your husband uncomfortable with it?'

'No. I mean, it is fiction after all.'

'It's great that he's an editor, that he's so understanding.'

'Well it's really no big deal.'

I'm having one of my good days. A day in which I don't find it difficult holding a conversation without making the other person feel troubled or uncomfortable. Perhaps it's more Shinagawa's doing than mine. I'm in a good mood to begin with. Then I down my champagne, which puts me in an even better mood, and then the delicious appetiser made my mood soar even higher.

'By the way, Miss Takahara. About that matter I mentioned to you the other day . . .'

'About writing something for you?'

'Yes. I was actually thinking of a novel rather than short stories.'

'What kind of thing did you have in mind?'

I felt anxious. Whenever someone asks me to write something, I start to feel nervous, then I drink too much to try and calm my nerves. Then I end up getting drunk and accepting the offer. This is exactly what had happened with Kobayashi – I'd begun with no intention of taking the job, then I got drunk and accepted it with gung-ho enthusiasm.

'I'd like you to write a work of autofiction.'

'Autofiction?' I say, and the words begin to feel real. 'Autofiction,' I whisper to myself again and the word feels more real. But no matter how real it feels when I say it, I still have no idea what it means. It is best to be honest in situations like this, so I ask him.

'What do you mean by autofiction?'

'Well, in short, it's autobiography-style fiction. A work of fiction that gets the reader suspecting that it's actually an autobiography. After reading your short story set in the plane, I thought that you might be interested.'

'So . . . you want me to write a novel in the style of an autobiography?'

'Yes, that's it. I was hoping you would write a novel as if it were your own autobiography.'

I don't understand what he means. And when I think how I don't understand, it makes me feel even more confused.

'Are you asking me to write about my childhood in the sanatorium?'

Shinagawa looks bemused, smiles, then says, 'Yes I am.'

But I've never even visited a sanatorium, never mind been sectioned in one. So in other words, the words that have just spilled from my mouth are fiction. A fiction that I presented in the form of a joke with the intention of making Shinagawa feel bad. But without hesitation, Shinagawa expressed his desire to read about my childhood in the sanatorium. So what is going on here? Regardless of my intentions, Shinagawa hasn't been the least bit offended by my words. I can't understand it. Am I falling apart? Or has Shinagawa fallen apart? My inability to understand which of us is falling apart causes a crack to run through my head into which hydrochloric acid gushes to melt away my brain. Am I just imagining things? If I'm not, then surely there will be serious consequences.

'You do know that I've never been to a sanatorium?'

'Of course I know that.'

Shinagawa's smile, Shinagawa's mask, etches itself deep into my mind. I feel that something deep inside him might be falling apart. That is why, through sitting face to face with him, I am starting to fall apart as well. It has all been going so well, too. I thought I was doing such a good job of holding a conversation, but here I am collapsing again. Shouldn't Shinagawa have thought it odd that I mentioned a sanatorium when I'd never mentioned one before? But instead, he'd simply said 'Yes,' then smiled. Not a grimace, you understand, but a normal smile. So what should I do? What should I do? I can't understand this person at all and I don't know if it is because he is too normal or because he is too weird. All

I know is that I don't understand him. I stare at him and I think to myself, *I don't understand. I don't understand.* My confusion running ahead, I wonder what I should do and whether this is love? I consider misinterpreting my confusion in this way, but there is really no point in basing one illusion on another. This isn't love. In fact, it is something so far from love that it makes for an interesting idea. But this isn't the time to be playing with such ideas.

'Mr Shinagawa, do you know about my past?'

'Well, I've read most of your interviews, so I know most of what you've said in them.'

'I have never once mentioned a sanatorium.'

'But you were joking, right? About the sanatorium?'

I'm convinced there's something wrong with him. He must be collapsing inside. Is he trying to put on the mask of a smile, get me to lay down my guard by asking me if I'm joking, then stab me when I do so? Is he carrying a spear with him? Under the table, perhaps? That must be it. What should I do? I want to check under the table, right now. But if Shinagawa knows I'm on to his spear, then he might draw it out and impale me. So what should I do? It's a life-or-death situation. Should I risk my life by looking under the table? Or should I pretend that I have my guard down, that I'm falling into his trap? My palms are getting sweaty. I reach for my glass. I raise my glass, all the while keeping my eyes on him, then I tilt it back.

'I was born in a village twenty-two years ago.'

'You were born in Tokyo, weren't you?'

'Well, there's a village that's actually in Tokyo. Didn't you know?'

'No. In what area?'

'Towards Oome. There's a village over there.'

'Are you sure that's not your own interpretation of the area?' asks Shinagawa, laughing.

My own interpretation? No, it isn't! A village is a village. The place is even called so-and-so village. That's the way it is. At least, that's how it is in *my* mind. When I was young, I used to look out of the second-floor window of our house towards Oome and imagine what life would be like if I'd been born in a village at the bottom of those mountains and lived with a grandfather who was a wood-cutter and a grandmother who did our laundry in the river. This was the first time I'd ever told anyone the story I'd dreamed up when I was a child, and now I was telling it as if it were true, so I was a little excited. But then, the idea that I used to imagine such things was made up as well, so I guess I shouldn't really be all that excited.

'So what was I talking about? Oh right, that I was born in a village. So I was born in a village. And almost everyone in the village was a relative of mine. It was one of those secluded villages.'

'Yes.'

'I was the only child that was able to leave that village.'

'I see.'

I can tell that Shinagawa doesn't believe my story. This is the first time I've been able to understand what Shinagawa is thinking. And it's a great relief to me, too.

I'm glad that I've been able to take his feelings into consideration when choosing my words and that I've finally guessed right.

'It's all a lie, of course,' I add.

'I thought so.'

We both laugh and I down my champagne. Seeing that we've finished the bottle, he asks me what I'd like to drink. I tell him I'd like wine or something, so naturally he asks me if I want red or white and I say that either would be fine. Finally I am succeeding in making accurate predictions. I predicted that Shinagawa would ask me what I'd like to drink, that I would answer wine, and that he would ask red or white. What is more, I even know what he is going to say next.

'You can certainly hold your drink.'

Bingo! I almost raise both arms in the air, but manage to keep them on the table – one folded over the other. I remember that there could be a spear ready to impale me the very moment I let my guard down.

I often imagine that people are trying to kill me. And by doing so, I can turn every day into a fight for survival. Nobody has a time or place where they are free from the danger of death. People forget that. People live their lives with the basic assumption that they will still be alive the day after. I can't live like that. A plane might come crashing into me at any moment and kill me. A truck might smash into me or I might suffer a heart attack, a stroke or even a subarachnoid haemorrhage. So I'm always standing face to face with the prospect of imminent death. I live with that thought in my mind. Am I strange? Shin once said that he wouldn't be able to go to work if he lived his life thinking that he might die at any moment. But I write and I work thinking that I might die tomorrow. I even have meetings like this one. I live prepared to die. And no matter whether I'm writing, giving interviews, loving Shin, being loved by Shin, believing that Smith-Smith exists, listening to CDs, trying not to hear the sound of the trunk or having meetings like this, I do it with the full weight of my life. I drink champagne with the full weight of my life. I talk to Shinagawa with the full weight of my life. I wait for the wine to be served with the full weight of my life. I live life with the full weight of my life. When people disapprove of the way I am, I don't think that it's bad. And even if someone approves, then, similarly, I don't think that it's good. Having said that, there is one person I don't want to disapprove of me, and that's Shin.

'I haven't been drinking for a while, so I can't drink as much as I used to.'

'Well, you seem to be doing just fine.'

'About the novel, can I have some time to think about it?'

'Of course. If you agree to do it, I'll support you in any way I can. If there are any obstacles to you writing this, please let me know.'

'What period of life did you have in mind? Childhood, adolescence, adult?'

'All of them if you like.'

Shinagawa smiles a confident smile. I feel that he is probably a fake all the way through to his bones, that everything he says is artificial. But I also feel that if I turn down his request, then he is sure to kill me with the spear he has hidden under the table. Shinagawa the artificial man. I'm not about to play into his hands. And anyway, I'm an artificial woman myself. I eat artificiality, I grew up on artificiality, I play with artificiality, I excrete artificiality and I even live in an artificial world. So Shinagawa had better not try to take me lightly.

'It might come out to be more than 2,000 pages,' I say.

'It could be a two-volume work.'

'But I wonder how many years it would take?'

'I'm willing to wait as many years as it takes you.'

I suddenly notice that Shinagawa's hands are not on the table. Perhaps he has the spear in his hands. Perhaps he is only pretending to have his hands around his thighs and knees and is actually gripping the shaft of the spear. What should I do? I desperately want to look under the table and I shake the tablecloth with my hands perched on the table edge. But I'm unable to take my eyes off Shinagawa. I can't shake from my mind the image of him spearing me the moment I glance down.

'Mr Shinagawa, if you were going to write a work of autobiographical fiction, what period of life would *you* choose to write about?'

'Me? I suppose I would probably start at around the time I got married.'

'Is that right? And how long have you been married?'

'Seven years. It was right about the time I was transferred to the literature department.'

I wonder to myself what I've been doing for the past seven years and I think of how my mind isn't what it used to be, which is a pointless thing to think.

But now Shinagawa must have read my thoughts as he's bending down slightly. So what should I do? Try to make a dash for the door? Is that even possible? Why did I take the seat at the far end of the table? Even if I were to make a run for it, I'd still have to get past Shinagawa. He is bound to spear me the moment I try to get away. What a game of survival life is. Every day I come face to face with death like this. The words 'memento mori' come to mind and I want to sing them out loud.

'Mem . . . en . . .'

'Memento mori?'

I stare at him and see victory in his eyes. And as I continue to gaze at him with my eyes wide open, I feel a smile spreading across my face that turns into a giggle. Hearing it, Shinagawa smiles sincerely and begins to chuckle too.

'All right then. I'll do it. Autofiction it is.'

I shake hands with Shinagawa and we toast with a red wine that's as thick as blood. We dine on Iberian pork and I nonchalantly take a peek under the tablecloth – but all I can see is the shimmering gloss of Shinagawa's patent-leather shoes.

* * *

'I'm home!' I call out and Shin comes out of his room. I put my arms around his chest and he hugs me back.

'Did you have too much to drink?' he asks, and I feel so much love for him that I just can't tear myself away. So Shin picks me up and practically drags me over to the living-room sofa.

'The red wine was delicious, so was the Martini at the bar we went to afterwards. And the Martini at the bar after that. What? What is it Shin? You know I'm crazy about you!'

'Thanks. Do you want something to drink?'

'Yes. Some water.'

He brings me a bottle of water. I take a swig and feel it flow through my entire body. My blue pedicured toenails glow under the fluorescent lights and for a second I think it's the water gathering in my toes that makes them glow that way.

'You've had too much to drink,' says Shin in a tone that's both fed up and concerned. But I find it so unbearably adorable that I kiss him and throw my arms around him. How warm he feels. Even the liveliest of conversations doesn't come close to the intimacy of physical contact. I'm a firm believer in touch. In fact, I would even say that I have very little trust in sight, hearing and smell. The only thing that counts is what the skin feels. I would even go as far as to say that you can't really know someone if you haven't touched them. I feel I can only have a connection with people I've touched. I know this maybe seems like a harsh take on reality, but in the end, what the skin feels is the only thing that matters. No matter how much you love someone, that love will never really take on true meaning until you touch. Without that touch – a caress or sex – love is meaningless.

As I hold Shin tight and try to get as close to him as possible, I feel like an amoeba. Through holding on to him, I'm holding myself together and stopping myself from just melting away. In fact, I wish I were an amoeba. Then I could completely envelop him, become one with him. Slither, squirm and be in love with him. I want to do all I can at this moment, treat it as if it's my last. To touch him as much as I can, to express my love as much as I can, to express as much love as possible, using every possible technique and every drop of energy I have at my disposal. Go on. Express everything you feel for Shin. Express your love. All of it. Express all of your love. You may die tomorrow. No, any moment now!

'I love you, I care for you, I really do. Let's be together forever.'

'We'll always be together,' says Shin as if to calm me and I grip his hands tighter. I feel our body heat merging. Our heat melting, one into the other. My hands, which are slightly colder than Shin's, cool down his hands. And his hands, which are slightly warmer than mine, warm up my hands. If only every part of us could continue to merge like this, to neutralise, our love to melt into each other and turn us into a single ball. A perfect sphere. What I want is for me to be red and for Shin to be blue. Then we'll melt together and we won't make a ball with a marbled pattern, but instead we'll be pure purple. Me and Shin. No. Rin and Shin. No. RinShin. That's what we should become. There'd be no need to distinguish between us. But even though these thoughts go through my head, I know I can't even unite the hundreds of millions of selves inside myself.

'How was your day today?'

'It was OK.'

'How's the manuscript coming along?'

'It isn't.'

'How many pages do you have?'

'About two.'

'You know what kind of story it's going to be?'

'No.'

'Don't look so nervous. You look like you're going to throw up.'

'I don't think I'm going to be able to do it.'

'Why don't you write something based on your own experiences? You know, like the episodes from high school that you wrote about in an essay once? I think it'd be interesting if you turned those experiences into a fictional story.'

'But I wasn't thinking anything back then.'

'That's why it would be interesting.'

I pull my face slightly away from Shin's chest and feel the air slip in between us. He gently frees himself from my arms and places his cigarettes and lighter in his breast pocket. I don't know if it's because of all the alcohol I've had to drink or all the cigarettes I've smoked, but I can feel my heart beating heavily and I worry that I might burst out in hives just imagining myself alone in the room.

'I'm going to go do some work then.'

'No!' I scream and Shin stares at me, a little surprised. 'No, no!' I continue, but he ignores me. 'Shin I want to be with you now! I really want to be with you now. Not only now, but forever. But especially now. I want to be with you now especially!'

'I still have work I need to finish.'

'What is all this work you bring home every day?'

'All kinds of work.'

It's a secret isn't it? You open your secret trunk, you betray me, and you create new secrets every day, don't you? You fortify your secrets with more secrets so that they grow larger and larger don't you? You're accumulating more and more secrets from me every day and turning them into a snowball of secrets, aren't you? In fact, you're just one fat secret aren't you? But I can't say any of these things that I want to. I have to maintain my balance by not touching on any of his secrets. And by ignoring them, by looking the other way, I can maintain the balance I need to live. Because without that balance, I'll die. But what does that mean? That I prioritise the part of me that puts my life first over the part of me that loves Shin? And as these thoughts are going through my head, Shin says, 'I'll be going then,' gets up and leaves the room.

I frantically look for my portable CD player and plug the earphones into my ears. Then once *Non-stop Euro*

Adventure comes blasting through the earphones, I turn on the stereo and play *Non-stop House Adventure*.

I sit down at my computer, wrought with frustration. I turn it on and click the document I'm working on. But it's happening all over again – all I can see are blocks of text! What can I do? In this state of mind, there's no way I can write anything, but the deadline is tomorrow. I feel like I've hit rock bottom. That is, until the music from the CD suddenly stops. I leap up for a second, but I'm quickly relieved to realise that it's only Smith-Smith playing one of his pranks. I tap on the earphones to send him a signal and the sound reverberates against my eardrums. But it's scary. I mean, what if Smith-Smith decides to turn off both the portable player and the audio deck at the same time? And what if I hear the trunk at that precise moment? The terrible thought comes into my mind that I might throw myself out of the window if I hear that sound again – *slam, whiz . . . splat*! And I imagine myself a broken mess on the ground. But what should I do? What should I do? I don't want to die, I don't want to die! I love Shin so unbearably much, but I don't want to die. To love is to die. If I were alive, I couldn't love. To love or to die. To love or to give up love. It is all so unbearable.

Adding to the portable CD player and the stereo, I play *Non-stop Classical Music Adventure* on my computer. I give up on the manuscript and open a new document to try and write something else. I place my fingers on the keyboard and wonder where my rheumatism has gone, as my fingers dance across the keyboard like they used to such a long time ago. The sentences still look just like blocks to me, but at least now they register in my head. Letters. Words. Writing. Non-stop. I can't stop. I won't stop. It won't stop. Non-stop.

Shin isn't coming out of his room. I glance at the clock on my computer. Almost four hours have passed since he went in there and I haven't been able to stop thinking of him all that time. But why is this? Why do I have to live my life bound by Shin, the trunk and Smith-Smith? Why does my life depend on a trunk? I mean, I could die tomorrow. But if I do, it should be the result of an accident or some kind of illness. Surely it is twisted of me to consider killing myself in reaction to the sound of a trunk. I tell myself again that I could die at any moment and I imagine being hit by a plane, run over by a truck, getting caught in a fire or earthquake, or having some sort of instantaneous brain haemorrhage. But instead, what frightens me most is the sound of that damn trunk. No matter how many CDs I'm playing at once. No matter how much I make myself believe in Smith-Smith. No matter how many precautions I take. I'm still so terribly afraid of the sound of that trunk. And of how it might make me die at any moment.

It's always been with me, this feeling of not wanting to die. And I'm sure this feeling will continue to stay with me. Then *clunk*! I hear the sound of the trunk shutting through my earphones. Why? How could I? How could

I hear that through my earphones? How? How? How? Was I going to die? No, I wasn't going to die. I know. I'm not going to die.

I stop typing and pull out the earphones blaring out *Non-stop Euro Adventure* from my portable CD player. My ears hurt. Using the mouse, I stop *Non-stop Classical Music Adventure* from playing on the computer. Now all that is left is to put a stop to *Non-stop House Adventure* on the stereo. Should I do it? Should I? I tell myself there's no need to worry and I pick up the remote and press STOP. A refreshing silence fills the room. Silence. Just silence.

I knock on the door of Shin's room, I hear a few moments of shuffling, then he opens the door.

'What's the matter?' he asks me with a perplexed look on his face. And when I look back at him I realise I don't feel love for him anymore. I want a divorce. The words slip out of my mouth and I see the trunk through the gap between him and the door. I think I see the corners of his lips move ever so slightly, but I can't say if they've turned up or down.

Now I sit in the silence of the room. My fingers and nails striking the keyboard make the only sound. Not a single *Non-stop Adventure* is playing. And on the sofa lies one quiet dog.

2

18th Summer

He stinks, stinks, stinks. Or does he? I'm not so sure. Just thinking that he stinks is bad enough, but questioning myself is making me confused. I can no longer tell if it's just my nose deceiving me or whether he really does stink. It's weird. I can't even tell what's true anymore. Perhaps he is stinky. He looks like he stinks. I look at the bald, shining head of this dirty old man, this *oyaji*, while thinking all this and I picture myself shouting at him, 'You stink!'

'Rin, what're your plans after this?'

'Well, I'll probably go hang out somewhere. Or maybe go home. Something like that.'

'Well then, let's go get dinner together.'

'Yeah, but I mean I'll be hanging out with friends or going home.'

'Oh come on. It'll be my treat.'

'But I'm really full up from snacking.'

'Well then, we can go for a drink.'

'But I'm *really* full. Really. I mean I couldn't even fit a bug in my stomach. Anyway, my friend's waiting so I'd better be off.'

The *oyaji* grabs my wrist as I stand up, saying 'Come on, wait a minute.' But I swing at him with my other hand, spilling a glowing shower of ash from the cigarette between my fingers. He pulls back his hand, startled, and I make off – squeezing through the narrow gaps of closely arranged tables and sofas until I'm back at Kana's side.

'Oh my god,' I say, wiping the wrist he grabbed. 'That's so disgusting.'

Perhaps overhearing Kana's laughter, the *oyaji* glances our way with an annoyed look on his face. But it's not as if this is some kind of hostess club. It's just a match-making club where you pay to enter. And here he is, some disgusting *oyaji* thinking he can pick me up. It pisses me off. Cheap bastard. But then, it's only this matchmaking club that keeps me from starving. So far this year, I've been scratching a living out of alternating between club Casa Noble where I get free admission; a karaoke box bar, Byokko, where they let me sleep for free; a friend's place in Shinjuku; and this matchmaking club called Cindy. This was where I'd been coming the most, as they provided free food, free drink and free karaoke, too. I also liked the fact that the seating for the girls and the guys was separated – so as long as you kept turning down proposals from the *oyajis*, then you could avoid speaking to them altogether and kid yourself that you were just hanging and having a coffee with friends.

When it was crowded with customers, like it was today, the waiter would often try to talk me into taking a proposal. In most cases, like just now, the *oyaji* would just want to go drinking. In other cases, a price would be offered to go on a date. Or for doing it once. Or the price of my panties.

But, not being interested, I'd pass these suggestions off with half-hearted responses – leaving the *oyaji* to pay the proposal fee and leaving me with a sense of annoyance as I got up and returned to my seat. But at least I'm not a prostitute. And that's why I never take proposals.

The doorbell sounds, followed by a hearty welcome of 'Irrashaimase!'

'God, it's busy today,' I hear Kana moan by my side and I glance over to see two suits walking in. I set down my super-large eight by twelve-inch mirror on the table. I remember falling in love with this mirror as soon as I saw it, thinking it would let me fix my make-up easily wherever I was. It was only after I'd bought it that I realised that size isn't all that matters when it comes to mirrors. But at least it's big enough to hide behind while I was putting my face on.

'They're so gross,' started Kana's clientele commentary. 'That guy's definitely a cradle snatcher and that one there's a narcissist.'

Kana's tanned skin looked more black than brown under the dim light and I felt myself wanting to tell her, 'You're kind of gross, too.' But when I thought about it a little more I realized I was probably looking pretty dusky myself, so I didn't bother to point it out.

'Don't look at them,' I tell her. 'They'll send over a proposal.'

But she ignores my warning and starts doing impressions of them and laughing.

'Take a look at that girl's rack!'

'Yeah, I don't actually come here to buy girls, you know.'

'Look, that one's checking me out!'

Thanks to Kana drawing attention to herself like that, it takes less than five minutes for a waiter to come across with two proposal cards.

Both of us circle the answer NEXT TIME and not WOULD LOVE TO then hand them back. But then a more experienced member of staff comes over who won't take no for an answer, so we gather up our stuff, brush the guy off and get out of there straight away.

'That guy was unbelievable!' says Kana, flapping the hem of her skirt to cool off. It is really hot after all. In fact, every year it seemed to be getting hotter, maybe because of global warming or maybe it's just me getting older. Either way, the thought is just as scary. Either way, I'm using up what remains of my life, ticking time off in daily chunks. But I know the only way to stop wasting away is to die and I hate my body for being a prisoner to such a simple but inflexible system. Already, I am aware of a laziness in myself that simply wasn't there when I was in middle school or high school. Back then, I could get by on two hours of sleep, while three hours and a sweet bean-paste bun would be enough to have me bursting with energy. Bags under the eyes? Bloating? Skin-whitening treatment? I can no longer ignore these things as my youthful energy fades. Just last week, I turned eighteen. And in a few months, Kana – who is still flapping her skirt – will be eighteen, too.

'Shall we go to Casa Noble?'

And off we head with neither one of us answering or taking the lead.

The heat makes us frown as we slowly walk along and on the way we ignore a scout who calls out to us. He's actually an acquaintance I sometimes talk to if I'm killing time waiting for friends and I've known him for a while. He was already in Shinjuku when I first started living my nomad existence. Then he disappeared for a while, but reappeared about a month ago. He once told me he'd worked in a host club in Kichijoji during his time away. This is, of course, typical of the sort of people you find festering in the red-light district – packing up and getting out, only to find themselves right back where they started. First they experience some sort of setback while working as a host in a club. Then they start working as a scout. If that's not enough to keep them in food, then they start work as a construction labourer. Somehow, they end up drifting into the loan-shark business. Then, at some point, they get the misguided notion that anything is possible and they try to make their comeback as a host. And from there, they're set up ready to fall into the same spiral again. Even for those who manage to get back and start again in their hometown, boredom sets in sooner or later and back they come. It seems there's always a flow like this among men.

I stand there waiting for the lights to change so I can cross. It's taking forever and I consider sending a letter of complaint to Shinjuku city hall.

'So when I flexed my muscles like 'Ha!' it made the cum dribble out of my cunt.'

I turn around and see Momo being forced to listen to one of Ran's tasteless stories. If Ran were in a movie, there'd be a subtitle when she made her entrance, saying something like 'Fucks anything that moves'. Needless to say, she is very popular among the dickheads who think of nothing other than sex. She doesn't care if the guy is ugly or hot. She probably doesn't even care if it's a man, a dog or a horse – as long as it has the sexual equipment. With this strangely graceful outlook she has become a famous sex queen, known to whip people up into joyful delirium or cast them down into self-loathing. In other words, she likes it dirty. But having said all this, I must admit that my conversations aren't necessarily any more meaningful than her foul episodes.

'Wow. Rin! Kana!' calls out Ran musically while running over. 'What are you guys doing here?'

'We're going to Casa Noble,' says Kana, unenthusiastically, her tongue hanging out from the heat.

'Really? Come on, let's go to a party instead. Let's go, let's go!'

I know that taking up an offer from the sex queen usually ends in a messy situation and Ran's hyper attitude is making me feel a little wary anyway. I turn to Momo and ask her, 'What kind of party is it?'

But Ran answers me instead, 'There'll be loads of hot men!'

So I don't get a proper answer and Momo doesn't say

anything at all. She just stays quiet like always, as if she's trying to make her body – which is a little plump to put it nicely, or just plain fat not to put it nicely – somehow appear smaller by staying silent. As she stands beside Ran, the contrast in their personalities is so different it almost hurts.

'Hot men, huh?' says Kana. 'But that's hot by Ran's standards, so I don't know if we can trust that.'

'I swear it'll be awesome today,' says Ran. 'And they're all your type, Kana. You know, in good shape.'

Hearing this, Kana immediately decides she wants to go. So I guess I'm in too. I'm still suspicious, but it's so hot and the green pedestrian light is already flashing, so I follow on right behind.

Ran tells us it's a bit far, so we wave down a taxi and the four of us pile in. I try to keep my eyes on the road so I'll know where we are, but I can't because Ran keeps talking to me.

'So, so, so, Rin, you had a long-term boyfriend before, right? Did your ex have a big dick? Really? Very thick? And it bent to the right? Wow, could he pee straight? So why don't you get a new boyfriend? Yeah? Do you think you're maybe asking too much? Are you looking for a guy with an extra thick one? A nice long one that he can keep hard all night?'

I pretend to listen to her gutter talk as the cars flow by. And while Ran gives directions to the driver, voices from the radio linger in my ears.

'The hat that my husband likes . . .' It sounds like a

counselling show, but I have no idea what they're talking about. Then, after ten minutes more, the taxi pulls up. I get out and stand looking around me until Ran gets out and points, 'It's over here!'

'Is this an apartment building?'

'Yeah, yeah.'

I look up and feel dizzy as I take in the height of the building. I notice that all the windows have the same colour curtains, so maybe it's one of those apartments people rent by the week or by the month.

I start to wonder if maybe we should just leave and try to catch Kana's eye. She catches my look, but she doesn't grasp the meaning – no doubt distracted by the prospect of meeting so many cute men. I wonder if we're about to step into some sort of orgy and I think of how I've always maintained some level of moral standards, despite my unconventional, nomadic life. Were my moral standards about to be shot to pieces? And all because of Ran? I feel desperate, worried, apprehensive, but I follow Ran nonetheless as she hurries us along.

As I wait for the elevator I make a mental note of where the emergency exit is. And when we arrive at the fifth floor Ran opens the door without bothering to ring the bell or even to take off her shoes – so we all follow in the same way, too. We pass through a hallway and enter a room where high-volume trance music and odd voices pierce my ears. There are more than a dozen guys and four girls – some sitting on the sofa and others dancing. Strobe lights flicker in time to the music from the four corners of the room and I hear Ran yell out, 'This is Rin, Kana and Momo!' This brings responses of 'Hey' from all around the room.

All the guys seem to be in their late-teens to mid-twenties. Eight of them are tanned black and six of them have long hair. I'm introduced to each of them, but as they all look so alike I quickly lose track of who's who. Two guys sandwich me, we sit on the sofa and a whisky is placed in my hand. I ask them if they have any gin or something else, but they tell me they're all out. It's an apology delivered with no sincerity at all and I hold my glass out to catch the strobe light, making sure there's nothing else mixed in there with it.

I reach out and pick up a piece of cold pizza from the table, smelling it carefully before putting it in my mouth. Whisky and pizza. It's like a recipe for being sick, the oil of the pizza mixing with whisky bitterness to make an awful concoction in my mouth. I glance around the room and I'm startled to see one guy sitting very still under the strobe light, like a doll or even a ghost. I steady my nerves and watch him carefully, but he doesn't move a bit. Eccentric. Strange. Why is he doing that? Why be so still? Why all alone? Why?

The guy next to me seems to be sneakily refilling my glass after every sip. Noticing me staring at the corner, he leans and looks at me while pouring.

'What? What's wrong, Rin?'

'What's up with that guy?'

'Oh him. Party-pooper. He was forced to come.'

73

'Who is he?'

'He's a nerd. Just a nerd.'

I tilt my head a little in confusion and the guy suggests I go and talk with him, suppressing a smile as he speaks. A nerd, huh? This guy. I think back to something Kana said when we ran into a group of nerds at a First Kitchen restaurant.

'You nerds are gross,' she said. 'You piss me off. Get lost!' But I think she might want to do it with this one. But then again, he doesn't look at all athletic, so maybe not.

So there I am, standing with my bag and a glass of whisky, wondering what kind of nerd this guy is. I'm hoping I can just kind of naturally make my way over to him, but I realise I'm walking in a straight line towards him, without taking my eyes off him for a second. Maybe it's because I'm concentrating on not spilling my whisky. But I guess it's all right – I left the sofa to go speak with him anyway. I shrug and stand in front of him. Then I sit down next to him and still he doesn't look my way. Finally he looks at me, noticing me for the first time when I lean in to look at his face. His eyes look nervous, but more than that he seems paranoid.

'Uu.' A sound escapes my lips, formed by my wanting to talk, but doing so before I've any idea of what I want to say. He doesn't respond and I notice a glass sitting by his side.

'You drinking?'

'Not really.'

'Not really?' I ask.

'What?'

'What?'

'What are you talking about?'

'Oh my god,' I say. 'I think you're the most awkward conversationalist I've ever met.'

'Me?'

'Yeah. Oh, so you understood me then.'

'Yeah. So what?'

'What do you mean?'

'Did you want something from me?'

'Not really, no.'

'OK.'

What is this weird feeling? It's like I can't hit anything solid. Like everything is made of the breeze. It's like I'm speaking to an alien, like being taken away to another world, like having the noisy trance music, odd voices and the smell of whisky erased from this room. Even the sensation of the glass in my hand is disappearing, being lifted away.

'So, are you a nerd?' I continue.

'No. Not me.'

'So you are . . . ?'

'What?'

'So what are you?'

'I just mean I'm not a nerd.'

'Oh, OK.'

Really? I think to myself. Really, you aren't a nerd? I bet you are. Aren't you? If you weren't a nerd, you'd have been surprised that I asked you out of the blue. Anyway, I was told you were by that guy over there, so it's not my fault. Besides, if other people are saying you are, then chances are that you are a nerd, don't you think? You just won't admit to it. No? So which is it?

I feel like I want to go on condemning him and accusing him, but it's also becoming a drag and I really don't care anymore. I take one of his cigarettes without a word and smoke it. I see ash dropping from the cigarette in his hand and I look around for an ashtray, but there's none to be seen. There are a number of cigarette butts on the concrete floor anyway, so I guess it's all right to drop my ash on the floor, too. *God, the music is loud*! I think to myself and unconsciously find myself saying.

'You listen to music?' he says, turning my way.

'Yeah, well, same as anyone does.'

'What kind of music do you listen to?'

'Um, like trance, house?'

'What do you like in trance?'

'What do you mean?'

'Like, DJs you like? Labels you like?'

'Oh, I don't really pay attention to that stuff. It's for dancing at clubs.'

'Oh.'

'A-ha! I've got it'

'What?'

'You're a music nerd, aren't you?'

'You should stop that, stop using dirty words like that.'

'Dirty words? You mean "nerd"?'

'Yeah.'

'Nerd, nerd, nerd, nerd, nerdy nerlalalalah!'

It's meant to be a joke, but by the depressed look on his face I can see he isn't taking it that way. It was something that just came tumbling out of my mouth during my weird high. But I don't want him to be depressed. I don't know why. But I feel I have to do something about it.

'I'm sorry. Are you mad?' I say to him.

'It's OK. I've decided to take your words as musical notes.'

'Is that something related to having perfect pitch or something?'

'I'm impressed you've heard of perfect pitch, being a Barbie babe.'

'I have perfect pitch, too.'

'Really?'

'It's the truth. I started taking piano lessons at three, though I quit a long time ago.'

'Why did you quit?'

'I felt . . .'

'Yeah?'

'I felt like my dead body was inside the piano.'

'I . . . see.'

'It's weird.'

'Weird?'

'Don't you think it's weird? A kid thinking something like that?'

'It's not weird,' he said. 'It could happen to anyone.

You only measure things against the societal norms, using words like "weird" and "nerd".'

'I mean, you too are part of society.'

'You're running the risk of having people misunderstand you,' he says.

'Yeah, yeah, yeah, yeah, yeah, yeah, yeah, yeah.'

His face takes on that depressed look, making me feel bad all over again. Why do I do things that make people uncomfortable? I knew it might annoy him by saying 'yeah, yeah, yeah, yeah', but I did it all the same and that's worse than if I'd done it unintentionally.

'Sorry,' I say.

'It's OK. They're musical notes. So how far did you get with the piano?'

'Up to Burgmüller. But I was abnormally untalented. Absolutely terrible.'

'So why are you a Barbie babe, despite having perfect pitch?'

'Well it's not necessarily like I want to have perfect pitch. Barbie babes and perfect pitch have nothing to do with one another.'

'Really?'

'Hey, we're conversing like normal people! We're understanding each other.'

'We are.'

'Come on, be happier!'

'OK.'

Why was he here? A very basic question pops into my head. Who, among the others, is his friend? I look around the room, but no one looks like they'd be close with him. I see Kana being half-forced to chug down her drink, while Momo seems to have made friends with the girls who were here before us, and she looks like she's having fun with them. Ran, however, is nowhere to be seen. I guess she probably went off to do it with the guy she'd tangled up with a while ago.

'So, aren't you interested in girls?'

'What? Do you want to do it? With me?'

'No, no. I don't like nerds.'

'And *I* don't like Barbie babes.'

'And Barbie babes can't have perfect pitch, right?'

'That's basically the case, yeah.'

I'm very comfortable with this guy and his relaxed way of speaking and I begin to wonder if he might really be an alien after all, because somehow in this threatening environment I'm losing my sense of reality and feeling like I'm in another world, but at the same time I feel very calm.

Suddenly, I hear a girl scream and I turn around. I see the girl who screamed being lifted by two guys and taken out of the room while struggling, but strangely I remain calm. Seeing the commotion, I catch Kana's expression twist slightly in fear, but she seems unable to awaken her drunken body. But even now, after seeing Kana in that state, I remain calm.

'Are they going to rape her? That girl?'

'I suppose so, yeah.'

'Oh.'

'Everyone came knowing it's that kind of gathering.'

'I didn't know. And don't you think it's weird, calling something like this a gathering?'

'You didn't know?'

'No I didn't. And that girl they took, she was struggling.'

'Can't be helped. Ignorance is a sin.'

'What? You're saying egg-on-rice is a sin?'

He pauses for a moment. 'Yeah.'

Of course, I know what he means. And I knew what he meant the moment I asked him that question. But I'm not voicing it. So does he know that I know? Is that why he doesn't explain further? I'd been tricked by Ran into coming here, but from his point of view, this was maybe the same kind of ignorance. That and not leaving when I looked up at the building and imagined an orgy might be going on inside. I guess that is a sin too. So maybe I can't even say I was tricked. And even if I'm raped here, then I can't really blame Ran. In the end, I am my own responsibility.

'Am I going to be raped too?'

'You . . .'

'What? Why did you stop? Were you going to say I'm not cute enough to be raped?'

'No, I wanted to say that because you're cute, you'll definitely be raped.'

'I'm not at all happy about this.'

He looks at me, saying nothing.

'But you can tell a girl she's cute. Even though you're a nerd.'

'You make it sound as if being a Barbie babe is better than being a nerd.'

'So I guess it's really going to be an orgy then?'

A cloud of depression settles on me as the conversation progresses. Rape. Forced sex. Everything that is about to happen here is depressing. But underneath it all, I feel happy that he said I was cute. Right here, right now, at the age of eighteen, I've discovered that it is possible to feel simultaneously depressed and happy. He has taught me this is possible. But I'm guessing depression will eventually win tonight.

'You don't want to be raped?'

'No. Not at all.'

'I see.'

'I don't.'

'It'll be OK.'

What does he mean? What will be OK? Why will it? How in the world can guys just blurt out 'It'll be OK'? I mean, it seems like guys have been saying this at inopportune moments throughout history. But as I consider this right now, it doesn't actually annoy me. For some odd reason, the very second he said it would be OK, I felt like everything *was* OK. I even feel like everything will be OK, even if I'm gang-raped by all the guys in this room. Maybe that's his thing. He can give you confidence without any grounds or reason.

In the meantime, I see Kana's camisole being stripped off. Hey, that's my bra! Why is she wearing it? Ah, it's the one I left at Natsu's place. I guess she just decided to wear it. But, we have different cup sizes. Why does she think it's all right to just use my stuff? And what is she doing – is she actually struggling, or is she putting on a show that's really a kind of invitation? I can't tell. It seems her body isn't obeying her orders anymore, but she's moving around forcefully nonetheless. I watch as a brown-haired guy with a tan takes off the bra and drops it to the floor. My bra hits the floor – like a thing of no value at all. Not even a penny. My bra has no value. I repeat the line like a melody, 'My bra has no value. My bra has no value.' And I watch someone twist Kana's nipples hard, like a knob.

'Ooouch!' she says, but it really doesn't sound like she's rejecting this at all.

'Let's go,' says the guy next to me and he stands up like it's a drag to do so – with a sluggish grandeur that belongs to the end of the world. I wonder where we're going, but I stand anyway, without speaking a word. Then suddenly a big guy appears out of nowhere and startles me. All this time I've been seeing, listening and thinking about what was happening in the room, but underneath I think I've fallen head over heels for this strange guy who's appeared out of nowhere, and I've lost all sense of the true world. Perhaps I never understood reality at all. This big guy is extremely realistic. So realistic it makes me doubt all reality beforehand. Comparing the two guys, I can tell this big guy is a great deal more buff. Not that the other guy is thin. But in comparison with this big guy, the other guy looks as if he is made of thread.

'Where you going? Not leaving, right, Rin?'

I think of responding to the big guy's comment with a joke, but he grabs my wrist, pulls me in and squeezes my tit in a single movement without grace or beauty – just a primitive grab for my tit. This is annoying enough, but even more annoying is the fact that my nipple is hardening from his touch. Then the other guy pulls my wrist from behind, leaving me in an awkward stance with my spine curved back and my tit still firmly in the big guy's grasp. In fact, I think it is because I look so awkward that the big guy feels bad and releases his grasp.

Then my guy from the floor steps in between us and says in a firm tone that isn't at all nerdy, 'I'm doing her.'

'What the fuck? You were ready to go just a second ago, but now you're taking the best?'

'I'll pass her on to you later,' says the nerd. Then he takes my hand and we leave the room. I glance back just once to catch Kana's leg sticking out from under a guy, kicking the table with the distinct slowness of a drunk. When we reach the entrance he releases my hand and unlocks the door. In the hallway, Ran's loud moans escape from a bedroom and echo against the walls.

'You should go.'

'Are you sure?'

'Yeah. You should go or they'll find you.'

'How about you?'

'I'll be OK.'

'How will you be OK?

'I'll just say you ran away.'

'My name's Rin.'

'You should go.'

'Will we meet again?'

'It'll be OK.'

What? Why? Why is it OK? I want to ask him, but I hear the bedroom door open.

'Bye.' I wave with one hand and open the entrance door. He raises his hand slightly in reply, then the door snaps shut behind me and I turn away. The hallway is empty, but the elevator takes its time coming up, so I take the emergency stairs instead – my high heels echoing with every step. It feels good and I run all the way to the last step. I leave through the emergency door – and though I feel like kneeling and raising my eyes to the heavens, I don't. I run to a main road and then start walking, relying only on a vague memory. A number of guys try to pick me up, but I don't get into any of their cars.

Sandals in hand, I walk barefoot for more than thirty minutes and when I finally recognise the city, a sigh of relief escapes me. I put my sandals back on and follow my regular route. Tired. Hot. I reach Casa Noble and think of how I only went with Ran to get out of the heat, but instead got into something much hotter. I run down the steps to the basement, on to the dance floor, throw a kiss to DJ Kazu, as always, hug Roman, the owner, throw more kisses to people I know, hug people I'm introduced to for the first time, and then I dance my dance.

The trance music cuts the air and golden lights illuminate the round dance floor. I feel that every part of my body is bursting with a life of its own – as a collection of separate organisms moving as they see fit. I feel so good I could faint. Sweat washes away the make-up, sweat washes away the perfume, and sweat washes away the sweat. I wish it would wash away even more – that it would wash away all the things that could never normally be washed away. I give myself entirely to the sensation of pleasure and it almost brings tears to my eyes. And without reason, without grounds, I keep thinking. 'It'll be OK.'

'Why did you lie to me?'

What is he doing? Does he think this is some sort of game? Is this fun for him? I don't ask him or peer over his shoulder at the screen. But I know. This guy doesn't play games. I know what he's doing at the computer. He's mixing!

'Why the hell are you mixing, you bastard? Can't you see my anger? Look at me! I'm showing my anger with my whole body! I'm this mad! I'm serious!'

I'm so angry that I shudder, but Shah still doesn't turn round, so I'm reduced to playing the part of a ludicrous girl talking to a guy's back. I know it's not his intention to make me look ridiculous, though. Shah isn't manipulative like that. He just isn't interested in me when I'm shaking with anger.

'I'm asking you why you lied, you asshole! Talk to me! Don't ignore me! You should die before you dare ignore me! Or you should kill me right now! Go on, push me out the window! Kill me now!'

'Look, can you keep it down?'

Without turning round, he shows the palm of his hand to me as if to say 'Stop'. But I'm so angry, I want to break his stupid hand. I want to snap it off with pliers, but instead I weakly give in to the repetitive rhythm of the trance music that he's been playing in this room for three days and three nights.

When it comes to music, Shah completely forgets my existence. Or perhaps he never really cared about me to begin with. But wait a second, I'm his girlfriend, aren't I? I feel a sense of self-respect start to well up inside me and I begin to lose my patience. *I* am the girlfriend. *We* are a couple. I can't hold it in anymore.

'We're a couple!'

'Yeah.'

'What do you mean, "Yeah"?'

'Miso?' he says.

'. . . soup?'

'Yeah.'

'Miso soup?'

'Yes, three.'

'Three miso soups? OK. Why three?'

He ignores me.

'I said, why three?'

'For Rin and for me.'

'And who's the last one for?'

'Yeah.'

'What do you mean, "Yeah"?'

'Yeah.'

'So what do you mean, "Yeah"? Who's the third one for?'

'Look, we need three, right?'

'That's why I'm asking who the fuck the third one is for! Don't be all vague and start blabbering shit. Are you fucking with me? Oh my god, you're ignoring me again. Give me a break! One second you're blabbering "miso soup, miso soup" and now you're ignoring me again. Your thought processes are no better than a monkey's! Or a chicken's! Go kill yourself.'

'I've got to go.'

'What do you mean, you've got to go? Where do you think you're going?'

'I'm going to Roman's to edit.'

'But you were mixing here!'

'How many times do I need to tell you? We don't have the equipment, so what I can do here is limited.'

'Well, whatever, but don't be blaming stuff on me. Your lying was what got me mad in the first place, remember?'

'I don't have time for this.'

Shah puts his jacket on and heads for the door. So I tackle him in desperation.

'I'm sorry. I was wrong. I won't get mad again, even if you do lie to me. So please, please don't be mad, please!'

But Shah just brushes me off, saying, 'It's OK. I won't get mad, no matter what.'

So I just stand at the door feeling anxious and insecure. And Shah turns around one last time.

'I love you, Shah. That's why I don't like lies. Just don't lie to me, please.'

'I'm sorry. I won't lie anymore. I didn't think you'd get so mad.'

'I love you.'

I run to hold him and he catches me, but with a nodding gesture, as if to say, 'all right, all right', like I'm some kind of nuisance. Then he leaves the apartment. I wave at his back and say, 'I love you', but I'm left feeling alone, empty, unfulfilled.

I go back to the room, stare at that damn computer and tears come to my eyes. Why do I always spin my wheels? Why won't Shah face up to how much I love him? Why? Telling me 'I won't get mad, no matter what.' What does that mean? Maybe he can't get mad because his emotions are all dead. He says he didn't think I would get so mad. Well maybe it's not my fault, but his for not being able to gauge other people's reactions. How am I supposed to trust his promise not to lie to me again? And why do I like him so much when he's so completely detestable? I know now I'll never be able to trust him again.

It was great when we first started seeing each other. Though I do feel sad when I think about the really early days. Our dramatic first encounter on that awful rape night. Our second encounter over a bowl of beef on rice at the less-than-dramatic Yoshinoya restaurant. What with him having the typical indecisiveness of a nerd, the whole getting-into-a-relationship thing and the me-moving-in-with-him thing had all been rather unilateral decisions made by me, while wearing my rose-tinted spectacles. I felt that as long as I was with him, I could be happy for ever and ever. I had no doubts about that. That's honestly what I felt.

When we first started going out, a DJ at Casa Noble quit, which was really perfect timing. So I introduced Shah and they hired him right away. I thought we could be together at home and together when we were out – all the time! And I felt that life couldn't get any better – a thought that even made me feel a little depressed. But as time passed by and we spent more time under the same roof together, I began to understand the true nature of the music nerd. Day after day, he'd have his face glued to that stupid little computer – playing the same song and mixing it over and over again. I stayed with him, even though our once- or twice-weekly dates had turned into trips to the record shop. Then, after all this, he goes and lies to me. Unbelievable!

It was just two days ago. I'd seen a beach resort on TV and I said, 'Look at that! Look at the blue water. I wanna go there!'

But as I sat there pointing at the TV, desperately trying to convey my desire to go somewhere together, Shah got up from his desk and said, 'Got to go.' Just like he did today.

So I asked him, but in a way that was half-joking, 'Where are you going? Where? To this beach resort, perhaps?'

And he said, 'Kazu's taking today off, so I have to DJ in his place.'

Now I didn't know this, so I told him to wait a minute, then I questioned him, but it's as if he'd turned into jelly or something. Like he can't be disturbed by me, anyone or anything. Then, just like he did today, he took off.

Then after that, I found that his stand-in DJ story was nothing but a lie. This is how I found out. You see, my phone rang yesterday and when I said, 'Ah, it's Kazu,' I noticed Shah becoming a little fidgety. So I asked Kazu straight away, 'Why did you take yesterday off and make Shah DJ in your place?' And the moment I said that, Shah, who was facing the computer, twitched. Or so I thought. Of course, Kazu then asked me what I was talking about, but I didn't take it any further. I just told him I must have been daydreaming and let it pass.

'Anyway,' said Kazu, 'my friend's having an event next week. Wanna come?'

'Yeah, yeah, sure,' I nodded enthusiastically, then I ended the conversation, hung up and started to interrogate Shah. 'Why did you lie to me? Where the fuck were you? Are you fucking cheating on me?'

He denied cheating on me, but he fell silent for a while. Then he came out with it.

'There was a record I really wanted, so I was looking for it.'

'Well if that's all it was, why the fuck did you have to lie to me about it?'

'Because whenever we go to record shops you always rush me to leave!'

Now that just made me flip. I felt my whole body

shake with anger and I started to feel confused and get hysterical. I kept asking him over and over again why he'd lied, but having felt he'd adequately explained himself already, Shah just turned back to the computer as if to say, 'I've fulfilled my duties,' and carried on mixing the music I'd heard so many times before.

Click, click, click, click.

'What are you doing? Are you trying to answer me with your mouse?' I yelled at him.

I screamed at him, then bit my sleeve in anger, but he still wouldn't turn around. So I continued going at him all night – yelling, howling, crying, accusing. Then just moments ago, he just released himself from my verbal attack. I mean, what the hell is up with that?

I'd like to take this opportunity to congratulate myself for showing the ability to accuse such a non-reactive person with such forceful vengeance. But congratulating myself won't bring the night back. And besides, I blurted out that I loved him and I begged him not to leave me. All of this because I want Shah so much. Maybe I should turn the accusations on myself – blame myself for liking him too much. But then, why should I? I could never lie to him and I haven't done a single thing wrong.

Yesterday, before Kazu phoned, when Shah and I were still friendly, we were eating fried dumplings. I picked up the plate to clear the table and I pictured myself smashing it on the computer. I didn't, of course. Instead, I stood there holding the plate and shaking, until it seemed silly that I was shaking from the fear of myself throwing the plate. And the moment I felt this silliness, I stopped myself and walked to the kitchen. After clearing the coffee table in the living room I stared at the corner of the room that was dominated by Shah's computer and turntable. I really wanted to throw out the two plastic bottles on his desk, but when I touch anything on his desk he stares me down. I wondered to myself, 'Are you angry? Why don't you show me you're angry?' But he never does. He just glares, like he has an unquestioning belief in the power of his eyes. That's the only way he expresses his anger. Or maybe not. Maybe he's not even capable of feeling anger. Perhaps he uses his glare as a tool to convey what he doesn't want done – no more, no less. Either way, I feel scared when he glares. I wonder if he might leave me. I wonder if I'm going to be dumped. I'm filled with insecurity and fear. So that's why I try to avoid doing anything that will make him glare – and why I didn't touch his plastic bottles, even though they bother me quite a bit. Eventually, I manage to shake off the thought of the bottles, though, and I head off to the bathroom to get ready.

As the cold water runs down my body, I think to myself, *I wonder why I hate to be lied to so much*? I was even wondering this as I screamed and yelled at Shah last night. He lied to me. He lied to me. He lied to me. Just thinking that makes a rage well up inside me that threatens to send maggots bursting from my body. But why? Why maggots? Because anger is similar to maggots. It multiplies in no time at all and quickly reaches an uncontrollable state.

But I can kill maggots at will. Whereas anger is something I can't kill, so I hate it even more.

Shah told me he lied because I pester him to hurry up when we go to record shops. But if records are so important he should have explained that importance to me until I understood his need to go there alone. So why did Shah lie to me instead? Perhaps he thinks I lack the ability to comprehend it all. So he thinks I'm incapable of comprehending! He thinks I'm stupid! I open my eyes wide and the shampoo rushes in to sting them. Now I realise that Shah's lie has sent me reeling beyond my expectations. And even if I try to calm myself down, I sense myself trying to act cool and that disturbs me all over again. It's a vicious downward spiral, a shitty loop that I'm caught in and can't find a way out. All the yelling and crying has left my voice hoarse and my eyes swollen and my spirits seem to be running at what feels like an all-time low. I know this, but it doesn't make me think about trying to cheer up. I'm in no state to go out, but I stick to my original plan anyway. Shah's set won't start until midnight, so I go to an event at Club Media before going on to see him at Casa Noble. I hate myself for sticking to the plan, though. I feel like a child. Why can't I be more independent, more honest, and just stay home because I don't feel like going out after our row?

'What happened, Rin? Your eyes are so swollen!'

Kana joins me at the booth and asks me the same thing everyone seems to be asking me since arriving at Media.

'I cried.'

When everyone else asked me, I just told them to shut up. But I tell Kana the truth. Although one reason for my doing so is that I know she will never stop asking otherwise.

'Why? Did you fight with Shah?'

'He lied to me.'

'Why?'

'He said he was going to work and went to a record shop instead.'

'What? Why would he lie about that?'

'I don't know.'

I lie to Kana because she is drunk and because she is wearing a sloppy smile and because the room is just too noisy to explain. This club just doesn't have what it takes for me to tell the truth. So I lift my sweating glass of watered-down gin and tonic and I scorn myself, thinking, *a cheap watered-down drink suits me well*. I touch the cold glass and it feels as if electricity is running through my hand. But I'm bothered by one contradiction. I just lied. Like Shah, I lied.

Even though I still don't understand why he lied, I did hear the reason he gave, so I lied when I said I didn't know the reason. As for me, I lied because the room is too noisy. Then I'd acknowledged to myself that I had, in fact, lied. So if I knew it was a lie, then it definitely was. I couldn't even convince myself otherwise, because to do so would be to cover a lie with yet another lie. Surely it would be best if I admitted that I lied – and if

I admitted why, too. I should say it's because the room is too noisy. Because it doesn't have the elements required for conveying the truth. After all, when Shah lied, he'd felt like the elements required for conveying the truth weren't there either. So what are the required elements anyway? Well, when Shah lied about his stand-in DJ job we were in the apartment. Just the two of us, passing quiet time. It's true that I was whining on about the beach resort at the time, but did that cause the required elements to be lost? He could have said the beach resort looked nice, but could I please stop going on about it for a moment? He could have told me he was going to the record shop – and that if I went with him, then I'd rush him. Was there a reason why he couldn't say that? No, there wasn't. I always, always accept what Shah has to say and I always respect and prioritise what Shah wants to do. So why did he lie? Did he think I was a girl who wouldn't accept what he said and who didn't respect or prioritise what he wanted to do? Did he think I would deny what he'd said or ignore what he wanted to do? Well, I guess so. That must be what he thinks. And if Shah thinks so, then maybe that is the case. That's all. Really? That's all? Well, yes. That's all. And in itself, that isn't a big problem. I really don't want to admit that we're the kind of couple for whom such a thing would be a big problem. So I don't acknowledge what Shah wants to do? In the end, that's just stupid. Wow, now I see! So I put down my gin and tonic, grab Kana's hand and run on to the dance floor. And after reaching the conclusion that my problems are rooted in my own stupidity, I lose steam and it's not surprising. After all, no one likes to feel stupid.

Shah is doing his set at Casa Noble and I'm dancing. I imitate a bamboo shoot and I pretend to be growing. I stretch my arms upwards with my palms held together.

'What are you doing?' says Kazu. 'You look ridiculous.'

But I don't care. I don't feel like dancing well to Shah's set since he lied to me. Then I consider how Kazu must be thinking I'm stupid, so I lie again, telling him, 'I ate bamboo yesterday.' And I carry on.

Kazu nods while dancing, and makes a funny expression. He's probably thinking that I'm not making much sense or something like that. But why should I bother coming up with an explanation for my bamboo dance? I mean, life is a joke. Life is made of jokes. Maybe I'm the only one who thinks this way, and even if I am then I don't particularly care. Actually, let me rephrase that thought. *My* life is a joke. And those who can't understand jokes simply shouldn't acknowledge *my* existence. That would be fine with me. I don't exist. Just keep thinking that. Eventually I will prove my existence to the world. But that's so stupid! How on earth can I prove my existence to the world? I don't even know if 'I' ever existed. I don't know if 'I' exists even now. This 'I' showered in golden light, making bamboo movements to Shah's trance music. No one would acknowledge such an existence. Even I don't admit to such an existence. So does that mean I don't understand jokes either? Yes. That's true.

After all, I couldn't let Shah's lie pass with a joke or a flippant comment.

I feel I've changed quite a bit since meeting Shah. The more I love him, the less casual I am in my approach to life. Before, I was living like a nomad, having become tired of guys and of life. But the second I met Shah, I started out on my journey back to being a desperate person. Now I'm a really serious person. Maybe that's why I dance my bamboo dance. And maybe it's why I want to continue dancing my bamboo dance. I want to grow, grow, grow, grow! I want to stretch up to the heavens. If possible, I want to grow about eight inches a day, or at the very least four inches. Can I? Please?

When I crash from too much bamboo dancing and tequila, Shah carries me through to the VIP room.

'Is it OK?' I hear Shah's voice near my ear.

It's not OK. I still detest that lie.

Then I hear another voice. 'Sure. Did Rin crash as well?'

I realise it's Ran's voice, not Shah's. So I take it she's hammered too. I guess she's also one of those people who tries to escape reality with bamboo, tequila and lies.

'Ha! It's you, Ran!' I say and Shah puts me down on the sofa opposite her, saying, 'I'll come get you when my set's over.' Then he turns and leaves the room.

'I'm so glad you showed up. I was getting lonely,' says Ran.

'So what's up? What lie did he tell you?'

'Lie? Who do you mean?'

I want her to joke with me and let it go, but my question is a little too direct to be just shrugged off. And I can't get angry at her and say, 'Just laugh it off, you idiot!' I think half of the problem with my comment is in my delivery.

Still lying down, I open my eyes slightly and see Ran's legs. This is the first time I've ever spoken to her while looking at her legs. Had Shah set me down head-to-foot with Ran to purposely instil in me the unique feeling one can only get from being alone in a room with someone and looking at their legs? If so, Shah is a very smart guy. Or maybe a kinky one.

'Ran, don't you just hate lies?'

'Yeah. I hate lies. And I really hate people who lie.'

Ran's response brings me some hope. Now I understand – maybe sympathy is what I'm looking for. I want someone to understand my suffering. I've been wanting to share it with someone. Perhaps that's what I've felt ever since being lied to. And maybe that's why I've spent the whole night, with my whole body, expressing my suffering to Shah. Although ultimately he'll never understand.

'This guy that picked me up the other day said "I've got a massive dick," so I took him to a hotel, but it was incredibly small. It totally killed it for me, you know? It was terrible. Of course, I did him anyway, but . . .'

I didn't mean that kind of thing, I think to myself and I look at Ran's big feet and her chipped pink pedicure.

'There's more. The other day, I did it with this other guy that picked me up. He said, "I'll definitely pull out before coming." So I was totally riding him and moving my hips like mad when suddenly he just says "Ahhh!" and comes. That totally hurt my feelings, you know? I mean I'm on the pill, but that's not the point.'

I didn't mean that kind of thing either, and I notice Ran's little toe twitch. I wonder what has crossed her mind. Why is she moving her little toe? Maybe she's waiting for the right moment to kick me as I lay on the opposite sofa. Maybe that's why. Or am I just being driven paranoid by this situation of having her legs in front of my face? But, wait a minute – even if she did try to kick me, surely her legs couldn't reach my face. She is tall, though. And she's got long legs. But could her leg reach over the coffee table and reach my face on the opposite sofa? Maybe it could. But wait. I know that I'm drunk right now, so I don't know whether I can trust my own sense of distance. As a test, I close my right eye and bring my index fingers together in front of me. But they don't touch and instead end up nowhere near each other. So I'm right. I can't trust my sense of distance. I think of extending my arm to Ran's leg to measure the distance between my face and her leg, but she might say, 'What the fuck are you doing?' and kick my hand.

'And there's more. I was, like, abducted the other day, right? I was thinking, "Well, I don't mind if I'm just getting raped," but then they totally gang-raped me. It actually felt kinda good, but then they threw me out in like a forest or something. The second they dropped me off, I was totally dumbstruck. I really thought, "This is the end of me!" But I ended up managing to hitch-hike my way back. I did the driver too, by the way. But, you know, he did take me all the way to Shinjuku and he kinda saved my life.'

Was the topic of lying totally lost? Or should I take this in a better way? After all, Ran must feel the need to talk about these events. That's it – I show respect for others. If I hadn't considered Ran's feelings, if I'd just gone ahead with what I wanted to talk about, then Ran would have had to keep her conversation inside herself, while being forced to listen to me. But of course, this could be a lie too. I do have things I want to talk about, but I just can't because she's blabbering on so fast and furious. So I'm holding back for the sake of others. No, that's a lie. I'm lying to myself. Shah didn't hold back what he wanted to do for my sake. If he had done, then he'd have been lying to himself. So is that what everything is all about: we do what we want to – even if it means lying to others? After all, that is being true to oneself, isn't it? Did Shah think it was more of a sin to lie to himself than to me? Is that it? Does that mean Shah loves himself more than me? Is that it? So it's not that Shah doesn't acknowledge me as a human being or think I'm incapable of understanding. It's simply that he thinks he's more important. Is that it?

If that's the case, then there's nothing more I can ask

from Shah. How can I even have said, 'I want to go to this beach resort'? But what should I do? I want him to be true to himself. So what should I do? I know! I should completely share Shah's values. Surely that way he'll show me the honesty he has towards himself. So Shah, if you want to go buy a record, you should prioritise that above me. That's the correct thing to do. That's the right thing to do. There is nothing more righteous than that. So if I think this way and if I show how I feel, then I'll be putting my feelings first when Shah goes to buy a record. Yes! If I have the same values as Shah, then it all works out. That way Shah will prioritise my wishes. Yes. I just need to ignore my own will and do exactly as Shah wishes. What's that? What kind of talk is that?

'So what's up with you, Rin? Did Shah lie to you?'

'Yeah.'

'What? About what? I *so* want to hear! Shah really lies? I can't believe it.'

Wait a second, her toes just twitched! So what's Ran plotting? She just totally twitched! So you're trying to kick me, are you? But wait. Can her leg reach me? No – first of all, why is Ran trying to kick me? And look at those stinky-looking boots on the floor! Is she really trying to kick me with bare feet that have been in those stinky boots? But why? What did I do? Are you against me too, Ran? This is too much. Everyone's trying to shut me out. No one respects me. No one has any respect. But why? Because I'm that kind of girl? But what does 'that kind of girl' mean anyway? A stupid girl? I mean, Ran's a stupid girl too. There's no one more stupid than Ran! Why would Ran try to kick me – one of her own kind? Is there some sort of rank separating us? I mean, no one would think about kicking a comrade, right? We're buddies, right? It's true that I don't go to orgies and now I'm with Shah I don't do it with any guy that tries to pick me up. I don't give or get head and I don't let anyone finger-fuck me either. I actually say stuff like, 'Seriously, like, give me a break' and I act ultra-conservative. But basically, other than that, we're the same, aren't we? I mean, I like sex. I'm the same as you, Ran! So why do you hate me so much? Why doesn't anyone like me? Ran's toes spread. Like fingers.

'Ran, you can spread your toes!'

'Isn't it amazing? Look – paper, scissors, rock.'

Ran does paper, scissors, rock with her toes. I have a bad case of paranoia. I tend to jump to the conclusion that Shah and everyone else in the world's trying to shut me out and discriminate against me. But maybe everyone's actually very kind and is trying to respect me, and only my overpowering paranoia prevents me from seeing it. The world is full of kindness. There's a part of me that really wants to believe that. But there's also a part of me that can't. The result is the world I'm in. As long as a single part of me can't believe it, then the world is not full of kindness. Yes, that's it – I measure the world. This is the world I live in. The world measured by someone else is not my world. That's someone else's world. And the number of worlds that exist is infinite. There's one world for every living person and my world is especially mean. That's all there is to it.

'So tell me. What kind of lie did Shah tell you?'

'Shah doesn't lie.'

There I go again! I lied again. I'm the same as Shah. I'm a liar. I'm a fool. It's not like the elements required for telling the truth about Shah's lie aren't here. There's still the thumping bass sound coming through to the room, but it isn't so loud that it hinders the conversation. I could have explained what kind of lie Shah told me, but instead I lied about Shah's lying! I've had enough. It's too much – lies and lies and lies and lies! I don't want to think about lying! I'm not going to think about it anymore! It's too much! But then ... not allowing myself to think of something, that only makes my problems worse.

Right now, my biggest problem is that Ran's leg is trying to kick me. I keep returning to this point time and again. And I never reach a conclusion. In this way, my thoughts are like a Möbius strip. The way I laugh through my nose while thinking this is ridiculous. I know it is, but I can't do anything about it. No, I mean, I would like to think there is nothing I can do about it.

'Rin.'

On hearing my name I look down. Ran is also looking down, staring at me. Here we are, two people lying head to foot, staring at each other. So if you were to draw a line indicating our line of sight, then we'd make the letter 'Z'. Ran reaches out with her hand and waves me over. I extend mine too and try to touch hers. But we don't touch. Our arms aren't long enough. So however hard we try and stretch, our hands just slightly miss. We both give up and flop our arms down onto the coffee table.

'Seems like we just can't reach each other.'

Hearing Ran's voice, a single tear escapes my eye. Still lying on my side, I press my palms together and extend them upward. Like bamboo growing sideways. Bamboo growing on its side. Bamboo extending sideways. Bamboo that can't look up, ever. Bamboo that can't see the sun. Poor thing. Bamboo. Grow. Grow! A bamboo that starts to grow sideways will always grow sideways. Ran's laughter echoes in the VIP room. I feel both saved and insulted. But perhaps I should think of the insult as the saver. But I purposely refuse to say that. I just felt both saved and insulted. But in the end, what do I care? I've already put it behind me. I'm ready to live my whole life as a sceptical delinquent.

Though I expect him to go to his computer and start mixing again, Shah lies down beside me after putting me to bed.

'I'm sorry I crashed,' I tell him.

'That's OK. I was wrong too.'

'About what? Lying?'

'Yeah. I feel bad. I should have told you the truth.'

'And you won't lie anymore?'

'I won't.'

'Promise?'

'Promise.'

'Is that a lie?'

'It's not a lie.'

'I love you.'

'I think my flaw is that when it comes to music, I can't think of anything else. So I get lazy about everything else.'

'Then try to become a more balanced person.'

'I'll try. But please don't try to deny my natural characteristics.'

'Characteristics or nerd-eristics?'

'I've told you this many times before, but using the word 'nerd' to refer to people who are serious about their music just isn't right.'

'But you are. Shah, you're a nerd. Nerd, nerd, nerd!'

Shah turns his back to me. I tell him, 'Hey, I didn't mean it. Shah, you're not a nerd. Besides, I like my nerdy Shah, so the word doesn't matter. It's OK to be a nerd, you know, Shah? . . . Shah?' I hug his back.

'I'm going to sleep,' he replies, his voice sounding muffled, the vibration of his words resonating through his back and into my breasts. I decide to respect his wish to go to sleep. So I don't say anything more and I don't bother him. But when I hook my leg around his, he pulls away. Why did I ever get together with such a loveable man! There's such a childlike purity in his love of music. It's as if he's so innocent, as if he rushes forwards without looking back when it comes to his music. And then there's the kindness he shows sometimes. What a lucky girl I am, being loved by a man like him. But come to think of it, isn't it so cute of Shah to make up a lie on the spot about having to do a stand-in DJ job? Just so he could go to the record shop? And to me, a regular at Casa Noble, who would surely learn the truth in no time anyway. He just wanted to go to the record shop so badly, but he thought he might be stopped if he told me the truth. He's like a child, telling an obvious lie. I should have dealt with the lie with friendly advice and an open heart. I should have been like a mother, like the ocean, like the earth. Shah would understand if I told him nicely. That's it, what I'm lacking is maternal instinct. Instinct to be like the ocean, like the earth. I need to have a big heart. So please, my heart, expand yourself. Expand to the size of a wide open space. Expand yourself. Expand me.

'What the hell? Seriously, come on, I'm starving here! Don't fuck around, you idiot.'

'Well you should have gone ahead and eaten.'

'What? Why would I do that? You said, "Let's eat dinner together," so I waited. And I've been fucking waiting and waiting. I'm so fucking hungry I'm banging my knife and fork together!'

'All right, all right. Look, I'm coming home now, so can you wait just a bit more?'

'So you're going to be late, huh? You never, ever take

me out – every day you're mixing, mixing, mixing, and then you think you've got the right to be late? If you'd spent some time hanging out with me every day or if you took me to a beach resort, then you'd have earned the right to be late.'

'Well you say I'm late, but it's not like we're meeting up somewhere. You're waiting at home, so you should have done something while waiting. I mean, you weren't just waiting without doing anything, were you? I couldn't help that I'm late. I had to stay longer at work.'

'Wow so you're turning it on me now? That's your speciality isn't it? Turning everything around on me. Well whatever. Just fucking hurry up.'

Petty. So petty. I'm such a petty human being. I know it. If I could expand, then there'd be no problem, but I just can't expand. I hang up the phone while Shah is in the middle of saying 'I'll rush home now' and throw it at the sofa. 'I'll finish at midnight, so let's go out for dinner.' That's what he'd said. It was a phrase inferring a date that was long overdue, but then when the time came he didn't call, he didn't pick up my calls, then he left me hanging on for another two hours. Then finally he calls me and gives me the dumb excuse that he 'had to work late'. So it's no wonder I'm angry. I did think about going over to Casa Noble myself, but decided against it, in case we missed each other on the street. So now I feel cheated out of those two hours and I want them back! But it's only natural that I would think this way. I'm not wrong at all. This time, this time I'm really not wrong. I'm right to be mad. I should let the anger in me build up, then fling it all out as I charge the accused!

You just wait, Shah.

'I'm home.'

Of course, as soon as I hear Shah's voice, I lose steam. He's my eternal weakness and I run over to hug him. How could I have ever felt any hatred towards the cute and lovable Shah – even if only for a moment? The poor thing was forced to carry on DJing after his shift, on the night he'd promised to go on a date with his girlfriend. It must have been difficult for him, too. He must have been thinking about me and wanting to call me many times. But I'm sure he was too busy on the decks, so instead he must have called the second he could get away to apologise. Oh, I thank you so much, my poor kitty!

'I love you, my kitty.'

'Can you not call me kitty?'

'But my kitty worked hard today, hmm?'

'I did and I'm sorry that I couldn't call you.'

'No, it's OK. But why did your shift suddenly get extended? Was someone absent?'

'Yasu was off sick.'

'They should have had Kazu take over.'

'Well, Kazu was going out for a drink, so . . .'

'You could have said that you had a date with your girlfriend.'

'Well, the owner asked me, so it couldn't be helped.'

'Well then, Roman could have spun the discs.'

'Yeah but he was behind the bar. It got really busy a little after midnight and it was really tough, really.'

Really . . . I can feel myself becoming annoyed as I speak, so I decide to end the conversation quickly. Letting my temper and anger run wild while questioning someone is a bad habit of mine. It's basically a form of self-destruction. Then Shah pulls out a plastic convenience store bag and I tilt my head to look at it.

'So what's that?'

'A snack,' he says, 'to carry you through until we get our food.'

'It's for me?'

'Well I thought it'd be tough for you to walk on an empty stomach.'

Seeing the chocolate in his hand, I burst into tears.

'I'm sorry Shah, I really bad-mouthed you and accused you. You're always looking out for me and then I go and say such stupid things. I really don't know why I do this. Really, why do I do this? I'm really sorry Shah, you know I love you. I really, really love my kind-hearted Shah. Shah? I'm in love with you.'

'Yeah, I know. Let's go after you have a couple of bites of that.'

After eating two pieces of chocolate, we head to an Italian restaurant. Not to Shah's work, not to the record shop, but to have dinner together, and it all makes me so happy that even the sweet taste of chocolate left in my throat makes me smile. I try to take Shah's hand, but he refuses saying, 'Like I told you before, it looks bad when you do that.' And just for a moment, I feel like all hell will break loose, until he offers me his arm instead and I happily take it. I'm fulfilled, enveloped in Shah's love and kindness. In the late summer night I feel the warmth of Shah's arm around my right elbow, and I think I might have glimpsed the future.

Tomato cream pasta, cheese, bacon salad and – last but not least – oyster meunière. I feel myself going hyper over all this delicious food, especially since it's been so long since we went out.

'Really? You're not going to eat that?' I find myself saying repeatedly as I stuff myself with food. I feel sorry that he only ate the salad, saying the calamari in the tomato cream pasta scared him and that he felt oysters were the scariest of all seafood. I'd completely forgotten that Shah couldn't eat seafood, so I'd gone on ordering whatever I liked. I ask him if he wants to order something else, but he just waves his hand and says he's not so hungry. I offer to cook him some frozen *gyoza* when we get home, but when we do get home, he says he doesn't feel so well, and goes straight to bed without even having sex. As for me, I'm not sleepy at all, so I just sit in the living room, dazed, reflecting on the day. Actually, when I say reflecting, I mean regretting. I feel I need to be sorry that I acted like a girl with a small heart – even if only for a second.

First, it's not good to lose control. But I do tend to lose

control. I have to remember that I'm dealing with Shah, so I need to remember that Shah is a different species – one that basically never loses control. That's why I should turn myself into an organism that doesn't lose control. So I should do away with what I am. But I don't want to. I want to be me forever. So what should I do? OK, I should create a new me – a me that never loses control. Ha! It's so simple when I think of it that way. And dwelling on that thought, I sit and stare at the plastic bottles on Shah's desk.

First, I decide that I'll never become distraught. At least not in front of Shah. Shah doesn't have the sophistication to deal well with a distraught girl. So when he's faced with one, I think he fears that he'll become distraught, too. So he just looks away. That's it. He doesn't become distraught, get angry or start to whine. So that should be my approach to him. But why doesn't he throw out those empty bottles? Look, there are four of them already. Don't they get in the way when he's working? Aren't they irritating? As I stare at them longer, I begin to feel a strong link forming between them and myself, so I quickly look away. This is another one of my bad habits – trying to find reason in whatever it is that I'm concentrating on. Of course, the plastic bottles and I have nothing in common. It's just that they bothered me for no reason, so I stare at them. Of course, there can be no connection between the plastic bottles and myself. There can't be. But if that is so, then why do they draw me in so much? It's not that we're looking at one another. It's only me that's looking. Is there a 'we'? No, there's definitely no 'we' in talking about the bottles and myself. There is me, and there are the plastic bottles. Was I thinking this way because I had some wine I wasn't used to with dinner? Is that why I was being drawn in by the bottles? Later, when I'm calm, I'll see what an eccentric thought this was. And with that thought, I head to the bedroom.

He mixes all day from first thing in the morning, then off he goes to Casa Noble at five. Seeing him off, I use my best sugar-coated voice to tell him that maybe I should go to Casa Noble after all. But Shah tries to put me off, saying, 'You should see your friends; it'll be a good change of pace.' So what the hell is 'a good change of pace'? Does he think I'm mentally disturbed? Anyway, Kazu's friend is having an event today. And though I've never met his friend, I asked Kana if she'd like to go along with me. Now I'm wondering why I'm going, as Kazu won't be there and, like I said, I've never even met his friend before. Was I stupid? And wasn't it really weird the way those plastic bottles drew me in?

'Rii-ii-ii-ng!' The sound of the doorbell turns me around. Maybe Shah has forgotten something. I try to suppress my excitement as I head for the door, but I can see Kazu through the spyhole. I open the door and he steps in without hesitation or invitation, so I purposely make an annoyed face.

'Yo!'

'What?'

'I've decided not to work at Casa Noble tonight, so let's go to the event together.'

'Well I'm not ready yet, so can you go on ahead?'

'I'll wait. So let's go together.'

'Letting you in to the apartment is like giving you permission to do me.'

'Wow, you've really changed since you've been with Shah, haven't you? You used to be so kind.'

I see a look of lust pass over his expression. Jesus, he's like a monkey! Does he really think I'd do him? I'm Shah's girlfriend, dumbass! The only reason I did you way back then was so I'd get free entrance to Casa Noble! Not because I wanted you! Don't you understand? I can understand why you'd want to believe that I wanted you. But the moment you really believe that, then you'll die, you fool!

'Oh yeah, I went out with Shah last night. Did Shah tell you?'

'No.'

'Yeah, we were like, haven't been out in a while, and you know that bar called Sabu? We went there, right? And we ran into Yuna and her friends there, so we had a drink together, but I felt bad because – you know how Shah's not really the socialising type. Well, I ended up having fun on my own, you know.'

'Is that right? Well he was kind of late coming home, so I was wondering where he'd gone.'

'Well, he kept wallowing in his gloomy mood until the end, then he left before everyone else.'

113

'Yeah, well, I guess he's just not a good drinking buddy,' I say and smile. Maggots are starting to crawl. Starting to crawl under my skin. Starting to crawl under my smile. I feel like I'm going to explode, then Kazu smiles back at me.

'Oops!' he says, then reaches into his pocket to grab his phone.

'Hey, it's Shah,' he says, raising the phone to his ear. 'Hey, Shah! Yeah, I decided to take today off. I'll have Yasu take care of my set, so it's no problem. He's not there yet? Should be arriving anytime now. Yeah, so I've come to pick up Rin. What? Come on, it's not like I'm forcing my way in to the apartment to rape her! Huh? What?'

'Is she there?' I hear Shah's voice through the earpiece. By 'she' did he mean me? Is Rin there? Was that what he asked? I try to understand from watching Kazu's eyes. What's Shah telling him? I can hear his voice very faintly, but I can't make out the words. Then suddenly, an awkward expression forms on Kazu's face and he glances my way, gestures for me to wait a second, then steps outside. And as I watch him go, I think to myself that this might be over. It might be over. I might be over.

'I've already told her.' I hear Kazu's voice through the door and I feel like I've reached the end. I'm no good anymore. Look, I've just become no good. So much so that I will live like a no-good person from now on. Can I expect your support? Will you vote for me in the no-good election? Please lend your support to the no-good person right here. The no-good person that I've become.

114

I could aim to achieve the ultimate level of being no good. I'll seek only things that are no good. It may be foolish, but it's a foolishness that might somehow be beautiful. But thinking of it as beautiful might just be my misconception. This is the wrong way to think. It's just my misconception. But misconceptions are what no-good people have. They have them and that's why they're no good. And as they allow such ideas to grow, they become even less and less good. To be no good is to be that kind of organism. Tears well up in my eyes and I push my hand down my blouse to bring my breasts together, to bring the line of cleavage to the centre of my V-neck rib-top. No-good people make cleavage. They become obsessed with making cleavage. I tug again to gather my breasts and my cleavage is beautiful. I gather the flesh from as far as my back, from under my bust. Squeeze it all together to make a full, round, complete and beautiful bust. They're my tits and everyone should want to bury themselves in them. Everyone should praise them and forget about my other parts. I'm not looking for admiration for my face, my hair, my legs, my arms, my spirit or my heart. But don't ever disrespect my cleavage, please. I'm a no-good person and no-good people place an emphasis on their cleavage. My cleavage is also something that no one would laugh at. That's why I make my cleavage. What if people did laugh? Then I would laugh back. If a young woman laughs, then I'll laugh back – she'll only be jealous anyway. If an older woman laughs, I'll laugh back – she'll be even more jealous. If a young man laughs, I'll laugh back – he'll be getting a hard-on. And if an older man laughs, I'll laugh back – he knows how much he wants to suck them. So why do no-good people push up their tits? Because cleavage is the one thing other people won't laugh at you for. And if they do, you can laugh back at them. The reason for making the most of your cleavage is the desire to acquire a kind of almost violent power – a power that only cleavage has. I mean, I could be angry if someone were to tell me that my face is ugly. Or if someone called me immature or said my hairstyle is weird or that my arms are flabby. But if anyone says anything about my chest, I can say with confidence, 'You got a problem with my cleavage?' That's why I push up my tits.

Kazu returns having finished the phone call, but looks slightly scared when he sees me staring blankly in the entrance.

'Shah was wondering where I was. He expected us to arrive at the same time.'

I stick out my cleavage. I know Kazu would never be one to make fun of cleavage. That's what I like about him. I'm stupid. I'm a fool who pushes out my cleavage. But is it OK to be doing this? I try to feel a little more demure.

'Don't look at me like that. You're going to give me a hard-on.'

So I push them out a little more. He'll never make fun of them. He'll never laugh. Because Kazu is a fool. Though I'm even more of a fool than him.

'I'm serious, you're getting me going. What happened to you?'

But I don't say anything, I just push them out even more. The next thing I know, I can feel a cool touch on my neckline. It's Kazu's hand slipping down into my rib-top from the neckline. I'm so glad to have my cleavage. It's like I'm never alone, because no matter how stupid or no-good I might be, I know my cleavage will never let me down.

I feel like I'm excluded by everyone. Hidden away, made fun of, laughed at. Everyone laughs at me. I know. Everyone's laughing at me behind my back. Nobody even thinks about me. That's me. I'm banished by everyone. They ship me away to a deserted island and everyone stands laughing at me from the mainland. Everyone points and laughs. Always. Always. They always laugh. I'm alone on the island, naked, and I'm always embarrassed. But I am able to draw Kazu over to my side. Everyone may well be laughing at me, everyone may well be looking down on me, but while I'm having sex I don't need to think of anyone. I can just think about sex. That's why I wished for the power of my cleavage and for the sex that starts with a hand down my top.

'Shah told me not to tell you about going out for a drink last night.'

'I know.'

'You heard?'

'Yeah.'

'Did he really think I wouldn't tell you?'

'He's stupid.'

'He is.'

And though I do so only in the weakest manner, I find myself able to laugh at Shah from my lonely island. I brush Kazu's cheek with my lips and a delicate pink line is left behind. Down along his neck and further beyond. I grab onto him as he tries to penetrate me while still standing and I feel a sense of nostalgia. Maybe because I haven't been with anyone else in all my time with Shah. Maybe because my pussy is crying in response to the different size and shape. The feeling of something foreign. I wonder if my pussy is feeling sad about being entered by a dick other than Shah's. And as a teardrop trickles down my thigh and traces a path to my ankle, Kazu pushes me down to the floor, grinding my pelvis against the wood. The sounds of him pushing synchronise with sounds of wetness and the tears just keep flowing. I feel sad. So sad. I'm suffering. 'Can't you hear me?' my pussy cries out to me. Why am I being stung by this worthless guy? How can you use me like this? Why do something so awful to me? It cries and begs for forgiveness. It asks me to please tell him to stop. Tell him to pull out. Tell him to get it out before he comes. He's going to use me until he comes! Why don't you listen to me? Tell him not to come inside me! Listen to me! I don't want his despicable cum inside me! I'm supposed to be a holy place! A holy place only for Shah. Don't let him desecrate me! Please stop. Just tell him to stop!

'Shut up!' The words come out mixed in with my moans,

118

which confuses Kazu, but not enough to put him off his stroke.

How dare my pussy rule my thoughts! Shut up! Shut up! You're just a cunt. Don't you fucking cry. Don't you fucking give me orders. Die, you nagging cunt, die! What are you to talk about morals? About love? Chastity? Are you fucking stupid? A fucking pussy talking about chastity? Well there's the tail wagging the dog! I mean, isn't that weird? Besides, how dare *you* – a pussy – give me orders! Really, you're some pussy. But you should remember your place. If you don't change your attitude I'll go nuts doing it with all kinds of losers – *oyajis*, baldies, guys with weird-shaped dicks. Is that what you want? I mean, you're just a pussy. Even my cleavage has more power than you. Think about it, it's not as if this guy saw you, got a hard-on, then decided to stick it in. He saw the face and the tits first. If you were just somehow placed out on your own, no one would even think of sticking it in you. Well, maybe I exaggerate a little. I guess there are guys who would. They'd do you like they'd do a sex doll. And there are guys who'd want to lick you. But it's still the tits, the face and the voice that gets them hard in the first place. So to tell you the truth, you're not really that much of a big player when it comes to doing guys. Of course, it would be quite difficult if you didn't exist at all. I'll admit that much. But you need to just take this and stay silent. I mean, what's your problem? Seriously. Why are you crying? Do you really hate it that much? Can't you just shut up and listen to what I say?

119

'No I won't shut up. Don't you see it's not really me that hates it? I only hate it because you do.'

What the hell is my pussy doing talking back to me? You're just a pussy! It doesn't make any sense for you to speak. Don't you think you're forgetting your place there? Getting a little over-confident perhaps? Besides, I don't hate it. But I do seriously love Shah. But do I want to be with him? Forever? Well, yeah. I do want to be with him forever. But in order for me to survive, I have to do it with this guy, so I'm using you for that reason. That's all there is to it. I mean, I wouldn't do it if I hated it. So I'm telling you, you're getting ahead of yourself. You're talking about love, chastity and all that romantic shit just to intoxicate yourself, right? Well don't get yourself drunk on all that romance, you fucking pussy! Have you ever seen yourself in the mirror? You have a horrible face. You look like an ogre. In fact, you're so fucking ugly that I have no choice but to shave you in an attempt to make you a bit more presentable. But even now you're still not a joy to look at. You're ugly. And ugly things don't have power. You have no power or freedom. You're a lower creation, which means I am a superior creation!

'You're just saying that. You know you hate it, too. You know you don't want to do this!'

Look, this has gone on too long – I don't want to be having a conversation with my pussy! So can't you just shut up? I've already told you I don't hate it. If I hated it I would have kicked this guy off me. I would have punched him and made him go away. So I'm not hating it. How many times do I need to tell you that? Enough is enough. No, no, that's not right, it's not right. You're right, I am hating it. The truth is I do hate it. What my pussy says is all true and I probably shouldn't do it with this guy. Because I don't want to. Because I really don't want to. I don't want to do it with anyone other than Shah. But I have to. I have to in order to survive. It can't be helped. It's necessary for Shah and me to continue in our relationship. Because I'll die if I don't do this. If I stay this way I'll die of loneliness. So I'm just trying to live. I'm trying to find a way to live. I love Shah and that's why I'm doing it – out of hope. I'm doing my best to endure this. So please, try to endure it too. Please, please, won't you endure it? This is the least thing you can do for me, my pussy. Please, pussy. Please?

'Oh you poor thing,' says my pussy.

What the fuck? Don't 'poor thing' me, you idiot! And just then Kazu releases himself on my stomach. What would happen if Shah came home and opened the door this very second? This thought crosses my mind, but I know he'll never walk in right now. No way. I know his priorities too well. His music comes first. His work comes second. I know I come after that, but I never expected to come after a drink with Kazu and a bunch of girls.

'Now go away. And don't you dare say a word to Shah.'

Kazu looks up at me from where he's sitting on the wooden floor, with regret and hatred in his eyes forming gradually out of a dumb, ecstatic smile. That ecstatic feeling. It makes everyone jump out of themselves temporarily and

I wanted to jump out of myself for a moment, too. Jump out of this skin that covers my body. Jump out of my terrible self. That's one reason why I did it with Kazu. But I never reach that point. He never takes me to ecstasy. So I can't jump out, no matter how much I want to. Not even for a second. I so much wanted to get out of my horrible skin. Take just my soul and jump free.

Shah arrives home at the expected time. He's scared and his worried eyes follow me as I move.

'Welcome home,' I say.

He looks at me like a dog that's been cast aside and ignored for hours. He sits down on the sofa, clutching a plastic convenience store bag containing the chocolate-mint ice cream that I'd asked him for when I saw him off earlier, saying, 'Don't forget to pick it up or I'll die.'

'I heard Kazu visited.'

'He did. I didn't want to go to the event after all, so he left on his own.'

'I'm sorry.'

'About what?'

I'm not sure why, but I feel like I'm listening to Shah apologise for the first time. But he's apologised so many times before, so I don't know why this feels like the first time. But then I realise. He usually begins with the phrase 'My bad . . .', but tonight he doesn't. He sits there with his head down and I stand watching with my pussy now silent. Just a minute before it had been whining over my thoughts with its cries of 'I love Shah! I want to be with him forever! I want him to stick it up me this second and cleanse me after that dirty fucker!' But now it's totally silent and shows no sign of speaking ever again. Hey, pussy? What's the matter? What's the matter, pussy?

'I didn't mean any harm by it,' says Shah.

'By what?'

'By lying.'

'I know,' I say.

But what do I know? What? That he didn't mean to hurt me? I don't know anything. I don't understand anything. I'm stupid. I'm no good and I even have conversations with my pussy.

'I'm sorry.'

'About what?'

We fall silent. All of us. My pussy, Shah and me. Hey, pussy, what happened to you? You were talking away just a minute ago. We were having a conversation, weren't we? About the great love you have for Shah? About how you like him so very, very much? About how you just love him so much you don't know what to do? We were talking about these things. Now your dearest Shah has arrived and you've just fallen silent. What's the matter, pussy? Are you embarrassed? Are you blushing? If you are, then stop it – people will think you're on heat.

'But if I'd told the truth, Rin, you'd have been angry, right? So you do see my reason for lying, don't you? I mean, I haven't done anything wrong technically, have I? It was bad to lie, but if I hadn't lied then you would have been angry.'

123

His nervous eyes dart around and I want to take another puff then flick my cigarette at him. But I don't. I'm a reasonable girl. I've managed to avoid crying, yelling, screaming or dying and I've kept my balance, too – simply by doing Kazu. I've done all of this for Shah. Because I love Shah. I know he doesn't like hysterical girls, so I worked out what I needed to do to keep my balance, then I went ahead and did it. I'm so admirable. I'm admirable, aren't I pussy? You're admirable too. You listened to me. And you let someone in that you didn't even like – just so that I could keep my balance. Both of us are admirable. You're admirable. And you're horny. So why are you so quiet now? I just made a joke. Don't you have a sense of humour? Come on, pussy! What's the matter? Why are you so silent?

'Rin, I'm sorry.'

I drag the waste-paper basket from the entrance to the living room and stop in front of Shah's computer desk.

'What's wrong?' he says. I turn around with his words and without letting my eyes fall from his gaze, I throw one of the plastic bottles into the basket. Immediately, I see his worry turn into annoyance. I throw the second plastic bottle into the basket. His lips draw in tightly. I throw away the third bottle. But Shah doesn't say anything or move – he just watches me. And as I throw the fourth plastic bottle in the waste-paper basket, Shah doesn't do a thing.

I glance down at the bottles leaking leftover tea into the basket. Then I go to the kitchen, bring back the *gyoza* plate and return to the desk. As I bring the plate up to my chest, he doesn't utter a word, he just watches. Then an impulse shoots through my hand and the monitor smashes with quite a crash. I indicate my handiwork with the palm of my hand as I tilt my head to him, but still he says and does nothing. So I pull out the hard drive and rip a handful of cables out with it. Then I raise it to the height of my chest as Shah continues to stare in silence. I swing it up, then down, smashing it into the wooden floor – a dull sound fills the room and plastic pieces scatter off in all directions. Though he stays completely silent, Shah stares me down. Stares. Me. Down. I think of how the ice cream is probably melted by now and I wonder what happened to the opinionated outbursts of my pussy. Where are you? Hey, did you die down there?

My hair is curled high on my head and I'm wearing large sunglasses. I'm in a halter-neck top with an open back, and I've got hot pants, fishnets, pushed-up tits and a confident pussy. My customised, immortal self could probably dance forever – going out today, partying tomorrow and drinking at another get-together the day after. But for now, my body is open to the wind as it finds its way among the Shinjuku skyscrapers.

I cancel my plans to attend an event and Kana calls me stupid. But that doesn't bother me at all. The thing is, on the way there I saw some dog shit on the street and it just killed my desire to go. That's all. I think that's all, anyway. Or maybe I didn't really want to go in the first place. Perhaps I was just using the dog shit as an excuse. But whatever the reason, I just don't feel up to it and it feels impossible for me to do anything. All the parties I've been to recently have probably left me exhausted. So I go over to the karaoke box, Byokko, with the idea of getting some sleep. When I get there, I spot a notebook that's never caught my eye before – a customer comments book. Do they really imagine this cheap love-hotel touch will help bring in the punters? I think how I could teach the store manager a thing or two about bringing in more business as I flip through the pages and already I find a few entries – 'The gin and tonic was weak,' 'I'll come again with friends.' What rubbish. How boring. What a load of rubbish. Everything is so idiotic, so boring. What the hell is this? Is this dull, worthless existence my life? I'm so worn out I can't even force myself to smile about it and tears roll down my cheeks. I don't even know what I'm sad about. So how can I be crying when I don't have anything to be sad about?

I'm not sad about anything. I'm not sad about breaking up with Shah. I don't even care about that. I have no emotions. So why are my tears flowing? I'm like a lunatic. What do I want? What don't I want? What do I wish for? What don't I wish for? What's my problem? Helplessly I turn a leaf and on a completely blank page I write, 'Faecal Vomiting Panic'. Now what the hell is that? It makes no sense at all. A part of me wants to laugh about it, but I can't. So I just sit there, helplessly, desperately facing the almost blank page.

The whole world has gone mad around me. Or perhaps I'm the one who has gone mad. No, but I'm so calm. It's a cliché, I know, but the speed of the world changing amazes me. I only know the world was sane up to the point when I fell asleep last night. Beyond that, I can't be sure. But even in this crazy new world, Shinjuku is Shinjuku. The scouts on 'Scout Lane' haven't changed much. But I can tell. Elements have changed. This is not the world I've been watching. I'm deeply suspicious that the road I'm walking on might suddenly turn into a trampoline, so I take each step with care.

The light on the main road turns green and reflexively I step out, before reminding myself of the need to be careful again. What if the world is doing fine, but it's me who's out of sync? Then even believing my brain when it tells me the light is green – even that might be dangerous! I strike the pose of a runner waiting for the starting whistle and look around. Then, when the others begin to walk, I start my race – then suddenly become aware that all the people around me aren't humans at all, but aliens wearing human skins – so their bodies can't be hurt if they're hit by a car. My legs feel like they're getting tangled and I glare at the cars to my left and right to make sure they don't move. Somehow, I make it across. Then strange music fills my ears.

'Bee-bee bebeebee, bee-bee bebeebee, pee-pee pepeepee, pee-pee pepeepee.'

It seems to be coming from about a street away and I rush over there to witness an unbelievable scene. With my perception of the world yesterday, I might have guessed that the Rio carnival is being held in Kabukicho. There are caramel-coloured women dancing the samba. Caramel-coloured men playing music with drums and flute-like instruments.

'Bee-bee bebeebee, bee-bee bebeebee!'

Everyone is filled with energy. The women all seem to be exhibitionists. The faces of passers-by are a collage of smiles and surprised expressions, with some speaking among themselves, others pointing here and there, and others joining in the dance. What would the 'me' of yesterday have done? If sober, I would have spat on the ground. If drunk, the bright gold colours would have made me puke. But as no one is doing either of these things, the world – as I'd predicted – is no longer the one I'm familiar with, but a world of craziness.

I squeeze my way into the crowd of caramel-coloured women and shake my hips. Shake-shake, twist-twist, shake-twist-shake. The samba music soaks into my body immediately and I think of going to live in a world called 'Rio'.

'Hey-hey! Yeah, ha yeah!' I call out and the dancers around me gather steam.

'Wippee! Ha-ha! Ha-ha-ha, hey!' I carry on in a deep voice and the dancers' excitement builds even more. I'm enveloped in the feeling that if a string were to break somewhere in my body, then I would fall to the ground in pieces, and this makes me shake and twist my hips to the limit. Shake-shake, twist-twist, shake-shake, twist-twist. As the music picks up speed, my hips move even faster. My hips. My hips! And when the rest of my body starts to give way as well, the music blasts its final beat: Boom! Boom! Boom! As soon as the music stops, a roar of praise goes up in my direction to find me still standing in my final pose.

Then it begins all over again: Boom-boom ba-boom! Bumpty-bumpty cha-cha!

Mixed in with the cheering, the music starts up. I don't know what to do – I don't think I can move my hips anymore. I feel like I might collapse on the spot and I balance there, at a loss. I'm still frowning with pain when one of the dancers takes me by the hand. She twists her hips for me, as if teaching me how, and I twist my whole body in response. She cries out, 'Hee hey!' Then she turns towards me and rolls her crotch and I do the same. Next, I turn to face the woman dancing behind me.

Boom! Boom! Ba-boom! Twist-twist, shake-shake. Boom! Boom! Ba-boom! Twist-twist, shake-shake. Boom! Boom! Ba-boom! Twist-twist, shake-shake. Once I've gone through dancing with everyone there, I slip out of the line with my body still twisting. Everyone eyes me suspiciously and I feel odd. Normally, I wouldn't have attracted this kind of attention just through a little twisting and shaking, but as I'd already guessed, the people living around me in this world are crazy. The next moment I notice that one of the dancers has placed a two-foot long gold feather so it sways out of the top of my hair. It makes me stop dancing out of sheer embarrassment and I tell my body to stop.

I'm holding the feather as I drag my feet to Casa Noble, the samba music still running through my head.

Cha-cha la, cha-cha, cha-cha.

I run down the steps like I'm doing the mambo, the doorman nods at me, then opens the door and I enter. I'm immediately hit with the sound of 'cha-cha-cha-cha-cha, cha, cha', so even in this crazy world tequila parties still exist.

'Tequila! Ha-ha!' I call out with the crowd. I sign up immediately for the tequila shot tournament and I prepare myself with the eyes of a killer. No one can come close to me now. With my hardened drinking skills, I blow away three guys and one girl and make my way up to the finals. By now, I have no idea how many shots I've downed. All I know is that my opponent is the bartender, who was serving behind the bar until now. I want to attack him and ask how come the bartender can enter the challenge, but instead I shake my hips at him provocatively and shake his hand.

'Cha-cha, cha-cha, chacha.'

I pick up the shot glass from the table.

'Cha-cha-la, cha-cha-cha, cha.'

I let it sway before my mouth.

'Cha-cha-cha-cha-cha, chacha.'

I swallow it in one go.

I throw the empty glass towards the corner of the booth, where it breaks into pieces and scatters.

'Tequila! Ha-ha! Yeah!' I yell to the ceiling, my body still gyrating.

But when I look to my side, my opponent is still going strong and he's dancing around. Everyone is dancing away and watching our challenge. I catch sight of the girl I'd gone up against just a moment ago, and from the corner of my eye I see her throw up shit-coloured puke into her cocktail. I watch her drink go from its original red to a dirty yellow, then the girl collapses. But my challenge goes on. I raise another tequila-filled glass, look around the dance floor, then down it in one.

'Burns!' I scream as the warmth hits my stomach.

Again, I throw my glass behind my opponent and it breaks into pieces on the floor.

'Tequila! Fire! Yeah! Ha-ha!' And I twist, I twist, I twist!

He's still shaking away, too. But why doesn't he break his glass? Maybe because he's the bartender? The smell of that girl's puke or shit or whatever it is hits my nose and after three straight shots I win against the bartender.

'I win! I win! I win!' I yell and everyone on the dance floor seems to rise up in synchrony.

'He-hey, hey-hey, he-hooy!' I sing and cheer to myself.

I make my way to the booth, the soles of my mules crunching as I go and I guess I'm walking on the glasses I just broke. I reach the booth and grab the microphone, attracting an annoyed glance from the DJ up there. Leaning out of the booth into the dance floor, I yell out 'I'm God!'

131

and a great 'Yeah!' rises up in response. Then suddenly, a sense of fear comes out of nowhere, so I draw a breath and hold it. Already the music is changing from the mambo to that song that goes 'That's the way, uh-huh, uh-huh.' I feel like I'm on top of the world. But that's the last thing I remember.

When I come to I'm lying on a box seat. I can't hear any music or people's voices and I raise my hand into my blurred field of vision, only to find that it's emitting light! But in reality my hand just *looks* as if it's emitting light. And why didn't they let me sleep in the VIP room anyway? I look around the empty dance floor and head off to the VIP room. When I open the door I see the bartender from the competition banging the girl who'd puked her guts up earlier. Then I see a girl in the DJ booth yelling 'I'm God!' and in a whooshing instant I leave my body behind and enter hers. My shoulders are shaking with excitement and emotion. I grab my bag, stand up, then slip between the sofas and tables – kicking a microphone to the floor as I do. But I don't care. I just push on and push my way out the door.

3

16th Summer

I was about three months into high school when I began to realise that I might have to repeat my first year. Since I'd been cutting class altogether for the years when I should have been in elementary and junior high school, this was the first time I'd actually received a report card in a very long time, so it felt even more of a shame that my grades were so bad. I'd made the unfortunate mistake of underestimating my school – believing that any school willing to accept me must be one fit for idiots. But once I'd enrolled, I found that it was just as difficult to move up a year at this school as it was at a foreign university, and that only about a quarter of students managed to graduate on time. Half the students seemed to drop out or transfer to somewhere else and a quarter of the students in my class had dropped out already. In fact, the emptiness of the classroom had been a major reason for my skipping most classes from the middle of the first semester. But it's not as if passing the buck will get me the credits I need.

Having lost interest in my report card, I shove it in my bag and lay down on the hot concrete. It is almost as if I can hear the sizzling of my feet, stomach, arms, and face – all the parts that my sports bra and shorts don't cover. Sweat streams out of my skin along with the smell of suntan lotion that I've been applying and reapplying, and I wonder if it's the sun or the scent of coconut that's turning my mind to mush. But no, it's the summer itself. I open my eyes wide like an animal after its prey, but the brightness of the sun makes me dizzy right away, so instead I roll over onto my back. Then I hear their voices and look up to see Kana and Moetto walking up the stairs. They've taken their time.

'You're late.'

'So-rry,' says Kana melodically. 'By the way, Mita was looking for you, Rin.'

'Why?'

'Probably something to do with your grades.'

Before I'd skipped out of the principal's end-of-semester remarks to come up to the roof, we'd been grimacing at each other's report cards. Kana at least has a hope of moving up to the next grade. I think of Mita's face – plain and bumpy with a complexion like coarse tofu. Picturing him in my mind, I can almost hear Mita delivering his lecture in his warm and feminine voice. There is no way I can face that face of his. Not at the moment.

'Now the first semester's come to an end, there's something I want to talk to you about,' Kana begins as she sits down beside me. But as she pulls suntan lotion out of her bag I stop her.

'Let's go to karaoke,' I say, and I slip on my camisole.

134

'But I wanted to get a tan, too!' she says, looking a little grumpy.

'You want to avoid the sun though, don't you, Moetto? You want to go karaoke, right? I mean, with your anaemia, you'd faint if we stayed out here, wouldn't you?' I rattle on and on like this for a while, then Moetto nods and Kana gives up and gets to her feet.

We took the elevator down to the first floor. And as soon as the door opens there's Mita's face right in front of us. I've been skipping his classes for about a week now, and his face looked more tanned than when I last saw him. 'See you next semester Mita!' said Kana in a cheery voice, and Mita smiled just for a second, the smile disappearing as soon as his small, single-lidded eyes catch sight of me.

'Did you see your report card?'

'I did see.'

'You're ditsy? I know that.'

'Right . . .'

'At this rate, you're going to have to repeat the year.'

A stern look comes over his face, but I'm in no mood to engage in a serious conversation. A phrase from some recent news programme pops into my mind: 'Kids these days are apathetic.' And though I don't know about kids in general, I know that I certainly am. Meanwhile, the sun-boiled blood courses through my body. The sun has evaporated my ability to think. The sun is a demon.

'You don't care, do you?'

'Well . . .'

'You don't, do you?'

'You know . . .'

'Well, like I say, if you don't make up your lost credits next semester, you're going to have to repeat the grade.'

I move in closer to him and ask if he'll give me the credits if I do him. But he says that isn't an option, so I wave goodbye and we leave. The walk to the karaoke place has never felt so long.

'Who wants beer? Who's having beer?'

I order three beers anyway, not really giving the other two a choice, as the air-conditioner pumps out stale air that smells of cigarettes, but is nevertheless better than the hot, sticky air outside.

'You stink of coconuts,' says Kana, pointing at me. I've adjusted the flaps of the air-conditioner so the breeze hits me directly, but in doing so I've apparently spread my coconut smell throughout the room. Kana takes out her deodorant and sprays it on me.

'Hey, it's not BO!' I grumble, but she refuses to listen. The deodorant feels nice and cool on my skin, though.

'By the way, the thing I was trying to tell you earlier.'

'Oh right, you were saying something. What was it?'

I turn to face Kana and think I glimpse nervousness in Moetto's eyes. I feel the atmosphere go tense and start to get a bad feeling. I think back on my recent behaviour to see if there's anything I might have done wrong, but nothing comes to mind.

'What? Did you get pregnant? Or try to kill yourself or something?' I joke, but she just puts her deodorant away without a smile.

'You know, Rin, how . . .'

But just as she begins, a guy arrives with our beers. Kana shuts up and starts leafing through the song catalogue and Moetto moves our mobiles and cigarettes to make space for the beers on the table. Feeling confused, I take a sip of beer. Then, after the guy has left the room, Kana starts up again.

'So anyway. It's about Yama.'

'Yama? What about him?'

'Well you know how Moetto likes him?'

'Yeah? Oh come on! You know I haven't done it with Yama.'

'Really?' Moetto suddenly joins the conversation. She sounds upset and she's glaring at me suspiciously.

'You know I have a boyfriend. And Yama's not even my type. It's not even as if Yama and me have been hanging out or anything. So it's like I'm being falsely accused here.' I shift uncomfortably in my seat. Moetto glares at me, eyes filled with hatred.

'So how did this even come up? Are you saying I've done something suspicious? If so, tell me what it is. Don't just vaguely accuse me. What kind of chat did you have that brought you to that conclusion? I've even been talking with Kana about how we could set you up with Yama, Moetto! I was being supportive! So why start accusing me?'

'Supportive? You kissed Yama the other day!'

'We were playing the King's Command game! It was a forfeit! Seiji made me do it, so you should blame him, not me! Besides, it wasn't even a kiss – we just had to pass an ice cube with our mouths.'

I hear the sound of pages turning and turn around to look at Kana, who started the whole thing, but she has her head buried deep in the song book. So here we are having this intense conversation and there she is just sitting there, looking as if she's about to punch in the numbers and start singing any moment. *You started this so you could at least bother to listen!* I think to myself while glaring at her, but she doesn't even glance in our direction. It's like it's nothing to do with her anymore.

'But you're always in contact with him, aren't you? Last time I saw Yama, all he did was go on about you!'

Why should I continue to put up with this? I'd already been falsely accused, put on trial and even sprayed with deodorant!

'Look, he calls me sometimes. That's all. I've never called him.'

'So why didn't you tell me he was hitting on you, when you know that I want him? That's so cruel of you. You've been going behind my back all this time.'

'No, it's not like that. I just thought you'd feel hurt, Moetto. And besides, I haven't even been coming to school much recently, so I didn't really have the chance to tell you. If anything, it's not betrayal, but kindness.'

'But even if you weren't coming to school, you still could have texted me or told me some other way. You're horrible. You betrayed me.'

How ridiculous. Kana is ignoring the whole thing,

Moetto is sitting with her angry face and I'm completely at a loss. I start to feel like I don't give a damn about any of it. I don't care. I just don't care. I don't care about anything. Why should I have to suffer over something I don't care about? I light up a cigarette and I really begin to feel like I couldn't care less.

'Besides, Yama has a girlfriend,' I say, and Kana looks up at me. It's a look of surprise, followed by one of disgust. She's probably thinking I've brought up something I shouldn't have. Moetto's sitting there with a look of total surprise on her face. She doesn't smoke, so when I exhale I glimpse irritation in her face. But the next moment, she looks like she's about to cry. What a drama queen. She's like the Woman of a Hundred Faces. I finish my beer while cursing her in my mind and stub my cigarette out in the ashtray. Then I place a 1,000-yen note on the table, stuff my mobile and cigarettes into my bag, and stand up to leave.

'Hey, wait a second, Rin!' says Kana.

'I'll text you,' I say and I go.

Outside, the sun is setting. The sides of the street are teeming with annoying pedestrians – no better than dogs that shit in public – all walking on tarmac peppered with black gum stains. The city looks the same as it always does, but for some reason today it makes me feel hollow inside. Why should I let this pathetic world drive me crazy? I'm like a wild monkey that's been caught and caged in a zoo.

After riding the train for an hour, I walk into a pachinko

parlour near Gato's apartment in Saitama. I manage to find Gato, who's already won a box of silver coins and I announce to him, 'I'm thinking of quitting school.' But because I've so many thoughts rushing through my mind, my words come out in the wrong tone, making the 'thinking of' sound like a provisional decision, or even making it sound as if I'm talking about someone else. Nevertheless, the words themselves clearly convey my determination to drop out of high school. But all Gato says is, 'Is that right?' And he doesn't ask me anything more about it.

'Damn it.' I curse my machine in what I think is a small voice. But as I can feel Gato staring at me from two seats away, I realise it was louder than I thought. Is he glaring at me? *I don't deserve that kind of glare*, I think to myself. *I've only been forced into this lowly penny-pinching existence through your becoming a debt-ridden, low-wage pachinko freak*. Ridiculous as it is, I find myself becoming irritated at the slot machines themselves. I know that if we go home as losers, we'll have no way of surviving until payday.

Behind me, I hear the fanfare of *The Emperor's Cup*, signalling that the guy who'd been on a roll had hit it big yet again. This kills any sense of motivation I have left and I beckon Gato towards me.

'This machine is just eating my coins. I don't think it's going to spit anything out for a while,' I tell him.

He takes some time to check the machine's data, then says, 'All right you can stop then,' and goes back to his machine. For a little while I walk around the store to see if there are any hopeful-looking machines and I talk with the other regulars. But I soon get fed up and take a seat on a bench in the break area, where I read a book for a while and text my friends every so often.

I'm certain that Gato is going to stuff all the money he has into that machine. It took only a week after quitting school and moving in with him to understand why he's so heavily in debt. And why he continues to play the slots anyway. He's addicted to gambling. I also know that I've gradually been losing my sense of money since I started living with him. The guy is mad. I have to keep telling myself that every day or his habits might start becoming mine. He said his 200,000-yen salary would be reduced to about a quarter of that after rent, gas, electricity, mobile charges and debt repayment, so we should use the full salary to make money before we paid for all those things. He has to be crazy to apply this fucking logic every month. And I know that once I stop recognising that, then I'll be done for as well.

I lie down on the bench and close my eyes. There's Euro-beat playing at a skull-cracking volume and it's stopping my mind from relaxing. I open my eyes just slightly in frustration and catch sight of Gato walking towards me. I start to sit up, thinking it unusual that he wants to go home so early, when suddenly, out of nowhere, he slaps me hard across the face. I'm dumbfounded. Shocked. Too shocked to say anything. And Gato is just standing there glaring down at me with hostile eyes.

'Wha . . . Did I? What did I do?' My voice doesn't even come to me, but I mouth the words and accompany them with gestures. But all Gato does is shoot me a disgusted look and turn towards the aisles of machines.

'That machine you were sitting at! It's on a roll!'

So does that mean he should hit me? I just didn't understand. I didn't think the machine would make any money, so I told him I didn't think it would spit any money out in a while. That's all. I haven't lied. And what about him? He checked the machine and told me I could stop. Pissed off, I walk over to the machine I'd been sitting at, where some smelly old fart is piling up the coins in his tray.

It's such a pain. Not so much the fact that I left the machine before its winning streak, but the fact that Gato will keep on reminding me about it for the next week or even the next month – the nagging, unforgiving glob of slime that he is. Although I must admit we could have gone to a barbecue restaurant for dinner tonight if only I'd stayed on the machine. Thinking this reminds me of how I haven't eaten meat for a long time and I daydream about the Korean-style raw beef at the restaurant just behind this pachinko place. I feel the saliva build in the back of my mouth. I'm starving!

When we leave the pachinko parlour we have just 320 yen between us. That's all we have to live off until Gato's next payday, which is a full three weeks away. I remember that we're all out of rice back home, but the thought no longer sends me into a panic. I've learned there's always some way to survive when you don't have any money. Gato is given a lunchbox every day at the pachinko parlour where he works, so he won't starve. And I can try to forget my hunger by drinking coffee and water and licking powdered coffee-creamer. If I'm lucky, Gato will bring me his leftovers from lunch. It's as if we're living a life of abstinence, of making ourselves go without worldly things. But our hunger has been brought on by our desire to get rich quick on the slot machines, so we can't really complain. I endure this life. And like someone who keeps running without knowing why, I continue to take whatever life throws my way. Of course, in my case I know why I'm doing it. But I pretend that I don't, because that's the kind of person I am.

As we walk back, I ignore Gato's sarcastic remarks. And once we're home, we take turns licking coffee, sugar and salt. He says salt-salt-sugar-salt-salt-sugar is the tastiest combination. But I think the simpler sugar-salt-sugar-salt order is best. But our pointless debate doesn't last long as I can never sustain a conversation with Gato. He's a man of few words and when I first started dating him I used to always wonder what he was thinking. I bet he's thinking of how he wants to play the slots and how we were so close to winning. He's thinking, *I'm hungry*. He's thinking, *Who can I borrow money from?* It was highly unlikely that he'd be mulling over abstract concepts like the end of the world, the mystery of life, or the furthest depths of the universe.

I met Gato through a friend. When I first did it with

him, he saw the cuts on my wrists and told me he'd make sure that never happened again. But it wasn't as if somebody had forced me to cut my wrists, or as if it was somebody else's fault, or as if it was something I'd done to express a suffering that I thought anyone could do anything about. That's what I was thinking as I buried my head in his chest. I'd simply done it because that was what I felt like doing at that moment. Back then, I thought life might be easier if I lived with a guy like Gato. And though I wouldn't describe our situation together as easy, I did think I was maybe fortunate to live this penniless life in which the only thing I thought about was how to eat the next day. When you're hungry, your mind slows down. I surprise myself by the way I can think that tomorrow will take care of itself. But that's how I've been living for the past two months since moving in with Gato.

I awake to the sound of shuffling next to me. I'm hungry – that's the first thought that enters my head.

'Shit!' blurts out Gato as he tries to push his arms through his ragged Kansai Yamamoto pachinko uniform. I guess that he's late again and I sit up and watch him throw the rest of his clothes on, grab his mobile, wallet and keys, and walk out the door without so much as a 'See you later.' I think how even a man of few words should be able to manage that and I lie back down. But as I do, tears well up in my eyes and I feel overcome by the sadness of being treated as if I don't exist – even by such a loser like him. He is a loser. He really is. But the fact remains that I live with him and my life revolves around him.

With a hundred thoughts running through my head and my stomach beginning to rumble, I close my eyes. But it's too hot to fall back to sleep and I momentarily consider turning on the air-conditioning. Then I remember how Gato said it would drive up the electricity bill and how he said you can always fall asleep eventually, if you stay in bed long enough. I wish I could forget his words and I roll myself into a ball. Then slowly, I lapse into sleep.

I awake with long panels of sunlight streaming through the gaps in the blind and warming my face. And when I get up, I'm hit by a hunger I can no longer ignore. I remember that we're almost out of sugar and coffee-creamer and consider my options. I know I still have 200 yen in my wallet, so I need something cheap but filling. Toast comes to mind, but just the thought of the thirty-minute bicycle ride to the supermarket by the station makes me feel faint, so I decide it would be better to just not move. I adjust the angle of the blinds and peer between the slats at the abandoned factories behind our building – remembering how I'd once thought I'd never get used to life in a place surrounded only by fields and factories. But I have done. I'm used to it, and I think how scary it is the way people get used to things so easily. Then I swallow two spoonfuls of creamer for breakfast. I gather the laundry and step out on to the balcony. Sweating under the bright rays of the sun, I start the twin-tub washing machine. Then I run back into the house and drink a glass of sugar water before I start cleaning the apartment.

Since moving in with Gato, household stuff like cleaning and washing has been a piece of cake. A piece of cake? I've never used a phrase like that before. Is my hunger starting to seep through into my choice of words now? Oh, what I wouldn't do right now for a steak.

'Get ready to go out!'

'Huh?'

'To go out.'

'Where are we going?'

'Just be ready. I'll be home in about ten minutes, so be waiting outside.'

That's all Gato says before hanging up. My head is still preoccupied with thoughts of meat, but I know Gato too well to imagine we'll be going anywhere other than a pachinko parlour. But what about money? He must have borrowed from someone, pushed himself further into debt with the credit place, or played the slots for someone else. But I know it's too soon for him to have finished his shift and then gone to the consumer-credit place or to play for someone else, so I'm pretty sure that he's borrowed. It's a thought that makes part of me reluctant to go, but at the same time it makes my heart dance to think there might be the vaguest possibility of meat for dinner.

When I go outside, Gato is sitting in the passenger

146

seat of a car I've never seen before. He points behind him, I slide into the back seat and the car starts.

'This is Mr Isumi,' he says, 'our manager.'

And I say a quick 'Hello', then fall silent. Gato isn't the kind of person to be concerned about me not joining in the conversation anyway. I don't know which pachinko parlour we're heading to, but from what I can hear of their conversation, I assume we're going to Max 2. I smoke a cigarette, pretending to listen to the two of them talk slots. And from the way Gato is addressing him, I'm guessing that this guy he's introduced as his manager is his immediate boss. The ashtray is full of one-yen coins for some reason, so I flick my ash out of the window.

'You're the only one that likes that machine, Mr Isumi,' says Gato.

'I've been betting my luck on that machine ever since I won 150,000 yen on it,' says Mr Isumi.

'Yeah, well I don't believe in luck. Playing slots is all about probability,' says Gato.

'No, you young guys place too much emphasis on that. Pachinko slots are all about passion.'

'Well you're certainly passionate about the game, Mr Isumi.'

Fortunately the sound of my snickering is drowned out by the radio. I squint at the wind blowing in through the gap at the top of the window and I flick my cigarette at the Toyota Crown in the oncoming lane. It misses and hits the asphalt. For the rest of the ride to Max 2 I remain silent. Then, when we arrive, I'm not even allowed to

147

play! I don't know how much money they've managed to borrow, but it looks like there's enough for the two of them. So why bring me at all if they aren't going to include me in the conversation or the playing? Gato takes a seat in front of one of the machines without even a word and I head over to the sitting area in similar silence. I pass the time stepping outside to talk on the phone or messaging with friends. For a while I read a book I've brought with me in anticipation of this happening, then some guy comes over and hits on me. I tell him to come back another time when my boyfriend's not here, then I smoke for the rest of the time until finally, about three hours later, Gato comes over.

'I'm winning,' he says, handing me a can of coffee. Then immediately he heads back to his seat. Still smoking my cigarette, I place the can of coffee against my cheek and stare down at my book. When you're with someone as useless as Gato, it's easy to be moved by even the smallest gesture, such as a crappy can of coffee. But I shouldn't start to think it's acceptable or normal to think this way. I shouldn't allow myself to be fooled. I know I'm being treated terribly and I tell myself I should take care never to forget that. I take a sip of the coffee, then put out my cigarette and reply to a text message a friend just sent me. I don't know how to put this, but everything in the world seems so dull.

By closing at 10p.m., Gato has made 20,000-yen profit, but he seems dissatisfied nonetheless.

'I was just getting on a roll,' he says spitefully at the

prize-exchange counter. Mr Isumi, on the other hand, is pleased with his 50,000-yen profit and overhearing Gato's complaints, he smiles and says he'll treat us to a *yakiniku* barbecue.

'That's what I like to see!' says Mr Isumi, watching me stuff my mouth with meat. I chew on the succulent flesh and wonder how anyone could really respect someone who pretends not to order side dishes out of modesty and instead keeps ordering more meat. Rice? Veggies? *Kimchi*? No thanks! I'll stick with the prime *karubi* and the Korean-style raw minced meat, thank you very much.

'I prefer women with a healthy appetite to those who always say they're on a diet,' he continues – smiling his lecherous loser smile at me, watching me stuff my starving body while I have the chance. It almost makes me lose my appetite. Almost, but not quite. So I smile back at Mr Isumi and take another piece of rib from the grill.

'It doesn't matter where we go. All she ever eats is meat,' says Gato.

'There's nothing wrong with that, given how thin she is.'

'She's got no shame.'

'Should we get another plate of ribs?' Mr Isumi asks me, ignoring Gato's disgust, and Gato falls silent. I wash down the grease from the ribs with beer and say, 'Let's get this one from Hiroshima,' fingering the menu with one hand while slipping the strap of my camisole back on my shoulder with the other. Looking pleased with himself, Mr Isumi calls the waiter over and orders three servings. I

149

reach over to take the last piece of meat from the grill. But seeing that it's a piece of loin, I decide to go for the steak tartare near me instead. 'It's someone else's money. Someone else's money. Mr Isumi's money. Gato's boss's money.' The more I repeat this mantra to myself, the better the food seems to slip down – especially that delicious *kalbi* from Hiroshima!

I sit in the passenger seat on the drive back home. I had been about to get into the back of the car when Mr Isumi, with his face like a dick, popped his head over the top and told me to sit next to him. I looked at Gato and he didn't seem too pleased, but he did nothing to stop me. So I have to listen to Mr Isumi's stupid dirty jokes for the half an hour or so that it takes us to get back – all the while feeling an intimidating air from right behind me.

'I'm really into this one girl at a pink salon I go to these days,' says Mr Isumi.

'You're such a pervert, Mr Isumi,' I reply.

'She's got amazing technique, you know. You should go get lessons from her.'

What gave this disgusting old guy the right to tell me to go get lessons from some dirty pink-salon whore? And why was Gato being so silent and acting like he wasn't even there?

'Me? I don't think so! I'm already good, so I don't need lessons.'

'Is that right?' chips in Mr Isumi with a lecherous laugh. 'So how good is she, Gato?' But all Gato gives in response is a vague mumble. Why can't you tell Mr Isumi that I always do you right? Or that my technique is out of this world? Gato with his stupid silence is really starting to irritate me.

'So what would you do if your girlfriend was a pink-salon queen?' asks Mr Isumi. 'Like if she was the girl that gave the best tongue in the place?'

I'm beginning to find his dirty mouth almost refreshing. At least, in comparison to Gato's pathetic, girly response where he forced a smile and just said, 'That would never happen.'

'You'd have to make a special request for me at the store then,' I say.

'Woah! I'd be a regular!' says Mr Isumi.

Finally we arrive at the apartment, wave goodbye to Mr Isumi and find ourselves surrounded by silence. Without a word, we walk into the apartment. His presence is as thin as the air when it's just the two of us. Or is it my presence that's as thin as the air to him?

'Hey you.'

'Wa?'

I hadn't expected him to begin a phrase like that, so my response came out incoherent. He'd normally just begin by saying, 'Draw me a bath' or 'I'm going to sleep.'

'What is it?' I ask.

'Stop that disgusting way of eating.' He glares at me, burning with hostility.

But I can't see what the problem is. Because we were eating in front of his boss, I'd made an effort to properly rearrange my chopsticks in my hand whenever I'd picked them up or put them down. I'd been careful never to point them at anyone. And I'd made sure never to open my mouth when I was chewing. So why did I have to be told that my eating habits were disgusting by a guy who always speaks with his mouth full, smacks his lips when chewing, licks his chopsticks and then rests them on his rice bowl? It makes me furious, but I manage to contain myself.

'Was I that disgusting?'

'Yes. And don't suck up to people like that either!'

'I wasn't sucking up, I was just going along with him. It's not like I was doing it because I wanted to.'

'I'm just saying you should act more proper. Stop talking such stupid and vulgar crap. It's like you're shouting out that you're easy!'

'Is it so bad to act friendly in front of your boyfriend's boss?'

'Well Mr Masuda's wife doesn't act like you.'

Oh right, that lump of fat. Nobody would want to hear about her being easy anyway. Besides, I was only *acting* easy; it's not like I really am.

'Mr Isumi's to blame too,' he says. 'Sexually harassing someone else's girl.'

'So why don't you complain to him, huh? Tell him not to harass your woman.'

Gato's eyes open wide and he glares at me. They're bloodshot. And hazy. I can see he's irritated. Very badly irritated.

152

'I don't want to say things like that to my colleagues or friends,' he says.

I just stare into space, aware that his bloodshot eyes are still trained on me. But if I stay silent, I'll only piss him off more and I know nothing good would come of that. But there are times when you just want to be silent anyway.

'You listening to me?'

'Yes, all right. So I'll never suck up to another guy or say things that make me sound easy, and I'll stop eating in such a disgusting way, all right? I'm sorry.' I really couldn't be bothered with this, but I thought he'd hit me if I talked back anymore, so I just did the smart thing and apologised obediently.

'Don't take that tone with me!' he snaps back, my apology having only added fuel to the fire. Then he waits for a while before muttering that he's going to sleep and slams open the sliding bathroom door. I hear the sound of his piss hitting the water as I stub my cigarette out in the ashtray.

'You'd better damn well stay here, or I swear I'll go kill that other guy!'

I try to say that I've never cheated on him, but I manage to hold my tongue. Then I think of how ridiculous he's being and I try not to scoff, but before I can take a breath my body is thrown to the floor. I open my eyes wide to try to see what's going on. His body's on top of me and his furious face is glaring down into mine. But I still can't help finding something comical about his seriousness.

'I already called the store and told them you won't be working there anymore. And if I hear from anyone that you've so much as stepped outside, then I'll kill you and the other guy, too! D'you understand? From now on, you stay home!'

Wooah! I quiver my shoulders in mock fear. But only in my mind. As I nod obediently, I wonder what would happen if I really did do that.

'The other guy.' I thought it was hilarious the way he referred to him like that – to the guy I'd had sex with in a car parked in the fields. It makes it all sound so serious, when all that had happened was that four months into living at Gato's place – once I'd begun to get tired of days that consisted of nothing more than housework and slot machines – Gato had turned to me after a fight and said, 'You know we don't have any money, so why don't you go out and get a part-time job?' At first I found even the idea of work irritating. But once I'd started, I also managed to find a little pocket of romance that allowed me the occasional escape from reality. I remember my name 'RIN' spelled out with tires on a snow-covered parking lot. The exhaustion of going back and forth to juggle between Gato and the other guy on Christmas Day. The sleeping pill I'd spiked Gato's sake with at midnight on New Year's Eve to buy me time with the other guy on New Year's morning. All those memories came flooding back to me. But I shouldn't be talking about these things as if they're in the distant past. I almost smile at my ability to put things behind me so easily, but I stop myself, knowing he'll hit me if I smile.

'If you leave the apartment, I will find out! So don't you dare go outside. D'you understand? I *will* find out if you go out.'

Gato gets off me and starts getting dressed. He puts on his shirt and slacks, transforming himself from Mr Abuse to Mr Pachinko Parlour Staff – looking cool with his little clip-on mike. Then he lights a cigarette and sits down beside me.

'Even if you do escape, you've got nowhere to go. And even if you go back home, I'll come and get you. I'm sorry, but I have absolutely no intention of letting us break up.'

Intention of us breaking up? Well I don't have any either! If I did, I wouldn't be putting up with this violent crap, now would I? From the very beginning I've only had eyes for you. And even though I don't like you that much, even though I didn't start going with you because I especially liked you, I've always put you first and followed you, I've always stayed three steps behind. OK, so I cheat on you sometimes. But even then I put you first. I've done everything I can for you. I cook meals for you every day and do other housework as well. All I did is cheat on you! And there's a good reason for that too. It's because you don't treat me right. All you do is play slots every day and you never pay attention to me. All you ever say is 'Draw me a bath' or 'I want my dinner' like some shitty husband. You even tell me how cute your friends' girlfriends are, so how can it really come as a surprise that I cheat on you?

I don't know why, damn it. I don't know why. It's not because you caught me and the other guy, then beat us both. It's not even because you carry on knocking me around and shouting at me all night. And it's not because you keep me prisoner in the apartment and won't let me out. I don't know, maybe it's because of all those things rolled together. But whatever it is, it's making me cry.

'You listening to me?'

I pout and nod at him. He strokes my head, stubs out his cigarette, puts his mobile and wallet in his pocket, and stands up. He'd already confiscated my purse and its contents last night. And he's snapped my mobile in two. He ripped the apron and blouse I use for work to shreds and left it strewn across the floor – the one I wore when me and the other guy were having role-play sex as a waitress doing her customer. All the racks, drawers and containers I've been using have been turned inside-out in a search for anything suspicious and their contents scattered about the place. As he said himself, Gato knew almost everyone in this industrial district. So if I do step outside, the information really will get passed on to Gato and I'll be killed. Well, not killed maybe, but definitely beaten to a pulp. I shiver at the thought of my every limb being twisted out of shape, as if I've been squashed into a rubbish bin. Then Gato leaves the apartment and I hear his keys in the lock on the other side. The moment I hear that, a deep anger explodes inside me.

I stand up and kick the door with the sole of my foot

as hard as I can – making a dull thud, followed by silence. But my anger doesn't dissipate, so I turn around and kick the glass door of the bathroom in the same way, causing it to shatter and crash loudly. It feels good and I smile in satisfaction. Until I hear footsteps outside, followed by the sound of the door being unlocked. He's back! Straight away he grabs me round the throat and starts throwing me round the room. Then he slams me down on the futon and his shoulders heave with his breathing. But all I do is close my eyes and think to myself what a pain in the ass this all is.

Soon he leaves the apartment again. I wait for about five minutes, then I start kicking and throwing everything in sight. But after about an hour of this I calm down and start doing my make-up. Apparently, being imprisoned has had no effect on my feminine desire to look beautiful. What an idiot I am. I feel so terribly fed up. But above all, I'm just tired. I imagine the word 'dazed' floating around this dingy ten-mat space and my mind wanders on to a lot of different things. Though I haven't slept a wink since the day before, my mind is very alert. Yet despite feeling sharp, it will only let me think about things in fragments, so I feel frustrated that I'm unable to explore any idea in depth. I'm just so fucking fed up and I take a sip of my coke. But even that's lost its fucking fizz! So now I'm even more fed up.

'Knock! Knock!'

I hear a rap on the door, but naturally I ignore it. If it's Gato, he'll use his key and house rules dictate I'm not to answer sales calls. Besides, I'm currently being held captive. I'm about to laugh to myself when I hear a muffled voice call out 'Rin?' So I stand up. I recognise the voice, but I look through the spyhole to check anyway, before quietly unlocking the door. Then I open it very slowly and Mr Tokita, a regular at Gato's pachinko parlour, slips through the gap as if he were an almost invisible man.

'Seems like you've got yourself in a tight spot.'

'Yeah, you could say that.'

'I just got a call from Gato asking me to tell him if I see you outside.'

'It's crazy.'

We talk quietly, but we use exaggerated gestures to somehow compensate. We have to keep our voices down because the walls are thin and if our neighbour tells Gato that a man has been visiting, then I'll really be in trouble. But Mr Tokita has been over a few times while Gato is at work, so he's well aware of the noise issue. I like Mr Tokita because he's a sharp, good-natured, quick-thinking guy. In fact, if Mr Tokita hadn't been Gato's friend, then maybe I might have cheated on Gato with him instead.

'If Gato finds out you're here, he'll come after you too.'

'Don't worry. I parked far away and nobody saw me coming,' he says, walking in to the room with a casual nonchalance towards danger. I watch him and start to feel as if last night's debacle might have been nothing more than a dream. I miss the Gato that used to get jealous and make sarcastic comments when we'd all go out and Mr Tokita and I would be all friendly. Mr Tokita lay down with his head on my lap, as if it were the most natural thing to do, and as I stroke his hair I begin to feel sad for some reason.

'He said, "She cheated on me,"' says Mr Tokita, his eyes still closed.

I trace back the events of last night one step at a time. After having sex in the car, the guy was supposed to drive me home before Gato got off work. But my phone started ringing while I was in the middle of giving him a blowjob. It was Gato saying he'd got off early and had come home and why wasn't I there? The call sent the two of us into a panic, but the guy managed to park the car a short distance from the apartment and I got out and waved goodbye. It was the kind of thing that happened quite often. Just a normal, regular situation when you're cheating on someone almost every day, really. But the moment I stepped out of the car on that day I heard a great crash, turned round, and saw Gato, who'd jumped off his bike and was running towards us at full speed. I hesitated. I didn't know what to do. Should I get back in the car and escape with the other guy? Or should I tell the other guy to get out of there, then make excuses to Gato on my own? In the end, I did neither. Although I don't think I'd have had time to do anything anyway. Gato dragged the guy out of the car and started pummelling him while shouting stupid thuggish threats like 'I'm gonna fuckin' kill ya!' It was too embarrassing to listen to and he only let the guy go after the guy managed to say, 'But I'm only a friend from work!' So Gato turned to me and shouted at me, asking what I was doing riding in the car of 'only a friend from work'? Then he accused me of cheating on him, came over and slapped me around, then locked me in the apartment.

The moment I heard the other guy say, 'I'm only a friend from work' any feelings I had for him instantly vanished. And when I saw Gato running towards us, I'd actually done nothing on purpose. I hadn't made the choice to escape with the other guy and I hadn't chosen Gato and let the other guy get away. I'd just let Gato and the other guy go at it, and let the other guy decide our future. If he hadn't said what he did, I would have probably left this apartment and escaped with him. But he chose to escape and the moment I saw that, I started to really think about the future. No, actually, I'd been thinking about it all along. I'd even prepared two options – what I'd do if the situation went one way or the other. I'd tested the guy, then, weighing my options, I'd chosen Gato over him. That's all there is to it. That's just the way I am. I always make others decide for me, make others take the responsibility. It's true that I'd been shouted at and beaten, and that I'm feeling wretched now. But it's also true that somehow the situation is turning out to be a convenient one for me. I've played it well.

Since I moved in with Gato, I haven't complained and I've acted like I accept everything he says. I made him dependent on me, then I cheated on him at just the right time. It's my revenge for the terrible way he's been treating me, and it's to be my way of increasing my power and status from now on. That's right. By enduring everything about him, by holding on, by showing him that decisions are all in his hands, I've been quietly laying the foundations for revenge and planning my struggle for power. If the other guy hadn't run away right then, our relationship would have simply ended with the revenge. But after seeing that guy react the way he did, I made a new decision. That from now on, everything is going to be a power struggle. Right now, I may be biding my time, waiting for my moment, but I have no doubt that I'll amass more and more power from now on.

'But I didn't. I didn't cheat on him.'

'I know that,' Mr Tokita says in a kind voice and just watching him brings tears to my eyes. Of course, I had set it all up. But even so, I'd been hurt by it, too. I felt the guy had abandoned me. That's how I felt. He'd just left me and ran away. He must have known that he left me to be shouted at, beaten, and for all kinds of horrible things to be done to me. But even so, he didn't strike back; he just ran away. Leaving me abandoned. Now, already, he's like a memory from the distant past. That's what I tell myself. But I guess my wounds haven't fully healed yet, and once I start crying, I can't stop.

Mr Tokita strokes my cheek. 'Everyone knows you're not the kind of girl to cheat, Rin.'

I don't feel bad about being consoled for a different reason than the one I'm crying about – it actually makes me feel like I'm getting twice my share of sympathy.

161

Anyway, I wasn't in a position to not take advantage of it.

'All this time, I've been doing everything I can for him!'

'I know, I know. You've been admirable. Doing the housework and preparing meals every day. Gato, on the other hand, never does anything. He's no good.'

I nod my head and hold his hands. I want something to lean on, because people can feel very nervous when they lose something that has been a part of their everyday life. I've been balancing with each foot on a different dick for the past two months and after losing one of the dicks last night, I'm starting to topple over. So now I have to do whatever it takes to regain my balance.

'I knew Gato would get mad at me if I didn't get home before he did, so I had no choice but to ask a guy at work to drop me off, that's all.'

Mr Tokita puts his arms around me sympathetically and I cry into his chest. Little by little, I feel my wounds are healing. It really makes a world of difference to have someone there to comfort you at a time like this. I don't want to end up with my back against the wall – the very thought of it frightened me. That's why I always prepare my escape route. I think about the future, I think only about myself and I live my life thinking only about my own convenience.

'If you want to run away, you should, you know,' Mr Tokita says. 'And if you manage to get away, you can go out with me.' Then he presses a 10,000-yen note into my hand and leaves.

So there really are people who'll treat you kindly, even if you don't have sex with them. It's a thought that touches me a little. But then, if he is really kind, he'd have already whisked me away in that shiny black Cadillac of his.

I know I won't escape. It's not that I can't. I just won't.

I point at the EXPLOSIVE STREAK sign that's been placed on my slot machine and Gato laughs in his seat next to me. His machine has a sign saying ON A ROLL. We've both been able to get seats at winning machines, as we queued early in the morning. We're going to eat meat today. We're having meat tonight. I'm not taking no for an answer. I'm not going to eat anything other than meat. I sit there discussing dinner plans with Gato like this and as the pile of winnings grows I ask him to buy me a new bag. Then after several hours I can't stand it any longer, so I rush to the bathroom and pull up my skirt. Every second is precious and I'm frustrated by the way the ultra-thin toilet paper costs me moments looking for the end of the roll.

It's been three months since Gato first confined me to the apartment and by now my house arrest has effectively come to an end. I'd done as I was told and caused no problems, and about one month into the detention I'd been given a mobile phone for good behaviour. After that I was allowed to contact my girlfriends, then pretty soon I was allowed to go out with them, too. Obviously, I haven't contacted the guy I've been cheating with, and my life has returned pretty much to the way it was before all this. Today is Gato's day off and we've decided to go out somewhere for a change, and although I was disappointed that the somewhere turned out to be a pachinko parlour, I can't complain now that we're on a winning streak.

I'm walking down the aisle back to my seat, but my feet stop as I hear a distinctive sound mixed in with the blaring music. I give Gato an enthusiastic slap on the back and tell him, 'The bell for the upcoming special just went off.' That's when I catch sight of a girl's name, accompanied by a love-heart icon on his mobile screen. He snaps his phone shut, tosses it into the coin tray and turns around, but I've already grabbed my bag and I'm off before I even catch a glimpse of his face. I run down four flights of stairs and frantically press the button for the sliding doors before stepping out into the dizzying sunlight. I'm so pathetically confused.

I keep running. Maybe because as long as I'm running, I don't have to think about anything. But by the time I've come up with that explanation for my actions, my arm is grabbed from behind and I almost topple forwards and my movements become stiff like a puppet's.

'Why'd you leave the machine like that? What on earth do you think you're doing?' He's shouting at me, but there's a hint of guilt in his expression as well. He must have realised I saw the message from his ex.

'Just go to hell!' I shout back and try to run off again, but he grabs my arm once more and drags me to the side of the street.

'You really think we can talk about this quietly here?!'
I say, trying not to shout and Gato shoves me into the
shutters.

'You're scum! Scum! You . . . you . . . you beat up my
friend from work just for being kind enough to give me a
ride home! Then you . . . you keep me prisoner in the
apartment! You don't allow me to contact any guy friends!
And all this time you're exchanging sweetheart messages
with your fucking ex! You . . . you make me sick with
your one-man act. You make me sick, you prick!'

Unconsciously I've ended my rant with a rhyme.
Probably because I can't convey the extent of my fury
without some sort of a buffer.

'Don't you talk to me like that!'

'I'll talk to you how I like. I'm breaking up with you!'

'Well, give me your mobile before you leave, then.'

'I'll transfer the memory, then give it back. In fact, I'll
snap it in half so you get two for the price of one!' I shrug
provocatively, but as I do his fist comes flying and sends
me to the ground. My face contorts as my hips hit the
concrete, but the pain somehow helps me regain my senses.

We're in the middle of a busy street and people are
stopping to look at us or pointing their fingers and
laughing. But nobody shows any sign of calling the police.
I don't blame them, though. I probably wouldn't either if
I were in their position. I wouldn't blame them even if
Gato were to beat me to death right here and now.

'Forget about transferring the memory. That mobile's
mine. Now get up.'

But he's the one that knocked me down, so I ignore his hand and glare up at him. He pulls me to my feet anyway.

'You just want to call all my girlfriends and stick your fetid dick into them, don't you?' I hiss at him as I'm getting up, which makes him let go and hit me again.

Thud!

My body slams into the shutters and I slip to the ground, twisting my wrist on the way down. This time the concrete cools me down.

'Look! There's nothing going on between her and me! I already told you, she got married. She's just having some problems with her husband, so I was lending an ear, that's all.'

How could I have spent a year and a half of my life living with a guy like this? How could I have had sex with him and sucked his dick on an almost daily basis? It baffles me. With the benefit of hindsight, it all just seems so unbelievable. I hadn't particularly liked him when we first started going out, but I never thought he'd be such an evil, perverted, boring, pathetic shit. I want to get rid of the hole that had sex with this scumbag. I want to scrub it inside out and soak it in disinfectant! I glare at him with a mix of rage and shame and at that very moment a memory comes back to me. A memory of a girl that he introduced me to before we started seeing each other. He'd introduced her as his ex-girlfriend. And after exchanging just a few words with her, I'd decided that there was no way I was going to get along with someone so much older and so ugly, so all I remember of her is simply that – she was older and she was ugly. How could I ever have imagined that I'd end up moving in with Gato, going into a rage about him texting her, then suddenly remembering her? But that's exactly what's happening now.

'I can't trust the words of a rotten prick.'

I'd been bent and moulded into Gato's shape. When I first slept with him, I'd been pressed to fit his shape. And when I saw the text from his ex, the anger of it reshaped me again, but in the opposite direction, so that I'll never be able to fit him again. And he'll never be able to fit me. I've gone from being something concave and accepting to something convex, protruding. Now I'm more of a penis than a vagina. So he and I will never again connect.

'Just hand over the mobile – I'm going to go cancel it right now!' he shouts again, this time with tears in his eyes – tears of rage, I guess. The concrete beneath is cooling my behind and I momentarily think how I might become constipated. Not that I've ever been constipated before.

'I bet you don't even know how to, you stupid prick,' I mumble under my breath. Then his sneaker rushes in and digs into my stomach. I hadn't expected him to stoop so low as to kick me when I'm down. I feel like the worn-out sole of his sneaker has pierced my internal organs and I almost throw up the doughnut I ate before getting in line at the pachinko parlour.

'I'll kill you if you don't shut up, you whore!'

'Yeah? Well who was the one sticking his fetid dick in this whore? Huh? Moaning and groaning with pleasure.'

But before I can finish, he pulls me up by the collar and shoves me back into the shutters.

'I'll kill you!' he whispers in my ear. There's not even a hint of kidding in his voice and I think to myself *Wow, this guy's really serious*, but still I find it unbearably hilarious. I always find it hilarious whenever anyone starts acting serious, wearing a serious expression or just taking their life seriously.

'You keep me shut away in that apartment, you tell me not to contact my guy friends, you snap my phone in two . . . but *you* go and stick *your* rotten dick into the rotten cunt of your ugly, old ex-girlfriend and cough your stinking, rotten spunk up her! Then, when I find that you're cheating on me, you get pissed at me, hit me, kick me and spit out abuse and threats like 'I'll kill you!' You make me laugh. I had no idea you were such a pathetic case. You're a complete joke. And you were such a bore, too. And not just an ugly one, but an ugly narcissistic one who checks himself out in the mirror whenever you think nobody's looking. You crack me up!'

Of course, I know I'm in no position to talk. I'm the one who cheated first, after all. I complained about him breaking my mobile, but I'd already backed up my data and I know that he probably wasn't cheating on me, really. But just the fact that he made me anxious that he might have – even if only for a moment. Even just the fact that he's been contacting his ex, while telling me I can't contact my men friends. That all makes him look like a frighteningly disgusting creature in my eyes and I simply lost control. Gradually, though, I realise my true intentions. My feelings are as clear as day now that I see them through my own eyes. I'm making myself get hurt. Doing it on purpose. The instant I saw the message I chose to go over the top. It's the stress of having been confined to the apartment. The grim reality of life at Gato's, with its boring routine day after day. The anger of being abandoned by the other guy. I'm relieving these frustrations by blaming them all on Gato. Even though the imprisonment, the dull everyday routine – these were things that I had asked for. I wanted to be tied down, to have my mobile snapped in two, to be confined to the house. I also knew that Gato wouldn't abandon me, even if he found out about my cheating, and I compared him to the other guy bearing that in mind. That's why I'd backed up my memory and stayed confined to the apartment, when I could have run away at any time if I'd wanted to. I'd stayed for revenge and for domination.

All I'd wanted to do was to put myself in a situation where it was easy for me to live. And while I was confined to that apartment, I was able to tell him 'You are responsible for me.' I'd played the part of a dumb, wayward girl and gave him the impression that I'd cheat on him again if he didn't spoil me, and in doing so, forced him to spoil me, take good care of me and drive himself deeper into debt to buy me things. I'd predicted all this when I'd been caught cheating. I'd seen a way to take the easy path. I didn't especially like Gato, but after having lived with him for a while, I'd slowly started to feel some affection towards him. I knew that if I ditched the other guy and stayed confined to the apartment as I was told, then my levels of power and status would rise above those of Gato. I knew he wouldn't treat me terribly all the time like he used to. I knew I'd come to control him as I pleased. So when he told me he had no intention of breaking up, I chose to maintain a relationship that was as mutually beneficial as possible. And as a matter of fact, during my grounding, I didn't have to cook meals, I was showered with gifts almost every week and I was able to take taxis whenever I had to go anywhere. Gato insisted that I stayed with him and I got something in return. Both of us were happy with that. But when I saw the text from his ex, I realised I'd lost my bargaining chip. I could only continue to get the things I wanted from him as long as he felt he needed me. I wouldn't be able to get them if he started to think he could break up with me and go back to his ex. That's why I was all flustered. I'd found myself in a tight corner. And I'd lost all interest – in Gato, who had made me freak out, in avenging the terrible treatment he'd meted out to me, and in the power struggle between the two of us.

'Look, I just don't care about anything anymore. So let's just break up.' There, I've said it. I feel like everything is just too much trouble now and I no longer care what happens. All I know is that I don't want to be here anymore. Gato must have realised I'm serious, because he's changed his tune completely and is telling me over again how much he loves me. But I lose myself in the crowd – beating a narrow path with my best victim voice. I reach the apartment and shove everything that looks like it's worth anything to anyone into a paper bag. I jot down the information in the new phone that I haven't already backed up. I take the mobile that's telling me Gato is calling and snap it in two, just as I said I would, then I head off for Shinjuku with my big bag and the paper bag slung over my shoulder.

I thought that everything would somehow work out, and actually everything did work out to some degree. I kept flying like a kite cut loose from its line. A kite that can keep on flying forever. It was a thought that made me feel good. After leaving Gato's place, I moved around from one place to another. I'd had enough of having a boyfriend and living together. 'You betrayed me! No I didn't! Yes, you did!' All that kind of talk could wait another ten years.

For now, I just want to enjoy the moment. Enjoy the fact that I'm drinking at this moment, that I'm dancing at this moment, that I'm laughing and having fun with everyone at this moment, that I'm doing any guy that I feel like doing at this moment. This moment is the only moment that interests me. I don't give a shit about anything else. This moment is all that matters now. Telling myself this, I binge drink, I strip naked in front of powerful ultraviolet tanning rays, I do anyone I want, and I shout

'Yeah!' without really knowing why. These are the stupid things that are important to me. I'm so disgustingly self-absorbed, but I live in a world where it's only natural to be this way. So it never really occurs to me just how disgustingly self-absorbed I really am. Living this way just feels natural to me and I keep wandering the streets of Shinjuku as if nothing in the world could ever be more natural.

I know that if anything should happen to me, then that thing will be entirely my own responsibility. Responsibility is something that just comes falling down on you – even *I* can accept that. If you climb into the car of a stranger, they may take you some place you don't know, inject you with drugs, rape you, then abandon you in the middle of a forest somewhere. If you go drinking with strange guys, they'll mix drugs into your drink, film themselves raping you, then drop you in the woods. Fortunately, I've not found myself in that kind of terrible situation so far. I've been hurt badly enough to be scarred, but never quite bad enough to be psychologically damaged. I've also been made to feel wretched many times. But I have no complaints. I know that my body – my skin, flesh, organs – will always have to take responsibility for my actions. And even if somebody does inject me with drugs, rape me, film it and then distribute it, I won't be mentally damaged. But I suppose if I'm gang-raped until my vagina bleeds, if I don't go to the hospital afterwards because I don't have enough money, and if I can never have children because of that, then yes, it's possible that I might become mentally ill as a result. I've chosen a life in which there is no place for excuses. A life in which I don't depend on or belong to anyone or anything. I'm living my life as a kite that has no home to go to. And that's what I want.

It was around the time that I started getting used to my nomadic existence. I was at the east exit of Shinjuku Station. Waiting. I caught sight of Kana, who was ten minutes late, on the other side of the crossing. I call out 'Hiya!' to get her attention and I can just about hear her call 'Yay!' back to me. We walk through the street of red-light scouts and Kana glances at every guy who tries to recruit us or pick us up, likening each one to a different animal as she passes.

'Gorilla.' 'Water buffalo.' 'Goldfish.' 'Mongoose.'

'But mongooses are cute.'

'D'you think?'

'Well, it's that animal that's ferocious, but has a cute squirrelly face, isn't it?'

'Isn't it that thing that looks like a hairy crocodile?'

'I can't even picture what a hairy crocodile would look like.'

'And it's got a face like a chimpanzee.'

'You sure?'

'Yeah. Didn't you know?'

'A crocodile with a chimpanzee's face?'

'Yeah.'

'I really don't think that's what it looks like . . .'

I wonder to myself if that's what they really do look

like, though I'm pretty sure it isn't. But then I wonder again if it is. I let these meaningless thoughts occupy my mind as we walk. We arrive at Cindy's, where we gorge ourselves on sausages and tuna salad until we're bursting with energy. The waiter keeps trying to get us to go sit with men who have requested our company, but we manage to fend him off each time and we leave the place about an hour later without having to talk to an *oyaji* even once.

The moment we step out on to the street, Kana says she wants the toilet. I say to her, 'Isn't it funny to say you want the toilet?' And we both crack up laughing while we walk to a nearby pachinko parlour to use theirs. As I fix my make-up in the bathroom mirror, I ask Kana if she's peeing or pooping. She says she can't believe I can be so annoying. Then we walk out between the aisles of slot machines and Kana shouts out 'It's so loud!' like she's suddenly lost her mind, and everyone turns around to look at her.

'You're the one that's loud!' I shout back, calling even more attention to ourselves, and we leave the pachinko parlour amid stares of disapproval.

The moment we open the door to Casa Noble, we're engulfed in a tide of dense air. It's always like that. The place is underground and the air is always heavy and smoky, but for some reason I always find the place comfortable and I'm pretty sure Kana feels the same way. As soon as we're in, Kana dashes off onto the dance floor. There's the usual air of excitement. The usual energy. The usual alcohol. Roman is in the DJ booth, which is unusual, and I'm dancing around in a fever, which is usual. I shout and jump, I twist and grind, I join the others on the floor as Roman spins out his trance tracks. I feel like there's 50 per cent more blood pumped into my body than before. I feel euphoric! Eu-pho-ric!

Then, out of nowhere, as I'm shouting and dancing, I get a sudden fright. The trance music continues to pound its consistent beat, every second without fail. But from somewhere else a new sound pierces my body. No. No! Something's going to happen to me unless I do some-thing! My entire body shivers with fright and my dancing becomes more intense. I'm so terrified of that sound, I know I'll have a heart attack if it strikes again. But even so, I find myself eagerly awaiting it. What is this fear?

'Fear!' I shout out as my legs buckle under my dancing. It feels so good, it feels so frightening, I want to die. Let my cries reach up to heaven! But the feeling only lasts for the first hour and I end up running out of stamina and collapsing into the box seat. I watch Kana as she goes on dancing so vigorously on the stage. She must be some sort of alien, I think to myself.

'Here you go.'

I look up to where the voice spins out from the trance music and there's Kazu standing with a gin and tonic in each hand.

'Oh, thanks,' I say, taking it and downing half in one go. I don't know if he's already finished his set, but he sits next to me and, for some reason, strokes my ass.

175

'Hey, do you know what kind of animal a mongoose is?'

'Listen, I'm thinking of dropping out of uni.'

'What are you talking about all of a sudden? Don't kill the mood with talk about that!'

'But I'm seriously agonising over it.'

'So why don't you quit then?'

'You don't leave a lot of room for debate, do you?'

'A mongoose isn't a kind of snake, is it?'

'It's just that, this is the only thing I'm good at. So I wonder if I ought to try making a living as a DJ.'

'Just stay in school.'

'Why are you being like that?'

'It's better to have something to fall back on, isn't it?'

'Well, yeah, but . . .'

Huh, what? I can't hear. What? Huh? What? I feel like cross-examining him, but I manage to bring it under control. The loud trance music is making my body float. I clink glasses as a toast and knock over Kazu's glass. The gin and tonic spills out on the floor, just missing him. Unfazed, he stands the glass back up and I notice his cheap-looking ring: a silver crucifix perched on his finger.

Kazu holds out his empty glass to me and we make a hollow toast. Then I light a cigarette and wave back at a friend on the floor. I can't remember his name, but I have the feeling we've met.

'Same goes for you, Rin. You're always hanging around Shinjuku. You don't have anything to fall back on, do you?'

'Not really.'

Not really what? I ask myself, as a song I really like starts up and my body begins to jingle.

'But then . . . I don't have anything to fall back from,' I say as I give in to the dance floor.

I shake my body like crazy and I can feel that last gin and tonic turning into flesh and bone. It's soaking in. My gin and tonic. Soaking into me! Gradually being absorbed, becoming part of me, becoming my energy. I'm grateful to gin and tonic for being my fuel. My driving force! Because without it, I wouldn't be able to move. My power comes from gin and tonic. Gin and tonic is my life. My beloved gin and tonic. Listen to that incredibly euphoric sound. Look at the dance floor, this endless stretch of land. See how the golden glowing lights make me shine like a god. I dance together with a girl I don't know and the gin and tonic turns to sweat. Soon it will form storm clouds that will cover this endless land that is Casa Noble and cast darkness across the dance floor.

I'm exhausted. I can't dance anymore. No, it's not that I can't. It's that I'm *not* going to. I don't even want to. Kana disappeared before I knew it and Kazu, who was supposed to take care of me, left around three in the morning.

'Thanks for everything,' he said as if they were his dying words. 'I'm sleepy.'

I go to crash in the VIP room, but when I get there I find Roman already fast asleep. And as I definitely don't want to have to do him, I have no other choice but to leave Casa Noble as the dusky sky turns blue.

I breathe in the distinct morning air, at once refreshing and gloomy, and walk along wondering where I might sleep. It seemed the gin and tonic hadn't all evaporated into the clouds yet, as it was still wiggling its way through my body. That's probably why I can't walk straight. I could go to Byokko's or Ran's or go wake up Kazu – those are the three options I narrow it down to. Then I call Kazu, imagining that Ran would probably have a guy over at her place anyway, but all I get is the answering machine. So I decide to call Ran instead, but her phone is out of reach. I really need to sleep on a soft bed or a futon tonight. I really, really don't want to have to face that narrow sofa at Byokko again. Then I stop in my tracks, realising that dream is not going to be fulfilled, not tonight, and I crouch down to the ground. Screw it! I could just sleep right here! I place a hand on the asphalt to check how cold it is and I'm startled by a shout! But then, that's Kabukicho – no shortage of noisy drunks at any time of the morning. I just don't have the energy to care anymore. Sorry Kabukicho. There it goes again, that shout! I realise it's getting closer and closer, so I turn around and there's an Iranian-looking man standing behind me. At least I assume he's Iranian. Maybe because of the dark skin, the white shirt, and shabby khaki cotton pants.

'Whuh?' The sound falls out of my mouth unconsciously as I sense something unnerving about him – this man not five yards away from me. As if in response to my voice, he lets out another shout. But what I think is just a shout seems more likely to be a foreign language. The desperation in his face makes me nervous, but I've no idea what he wants, what he's trying to tell me or why he looks so desperate. Under normal circumstances I think I would have ignored him, but instead I find myself unable to shift my glare from his wide-open eyes.

'What?' I say.

Feeling uncomfortable crouched on the ground, I slowly stand up, supporting my aching knees with my hand. Then I see something shiny in his hand and the pain vanishes instantly. It's a knife! This guy talking to me is holding a knife! Through the immediate confusion and bewilderment, my body senses the danger and sends me running. I hear the same shout behind me and I turn around to see him chasing right behind. But not just chasing me – pointing that knife right at me like I'm his prey. A knifepoint seven yards away from my back. There are always, always people on this street, always, so why isn't there anyone here now?! I know I can run faster if I don't look back, but I can't help it. Shit! Shit! Shit! Don't look back, don't look back! You'll get stabbed! He'll stab you! Just run, run, run! Don't look back! Run faster! His footsteps are clear in my ears and I'm sticky with sweat. Shit! Faster! Faster! Run faster! You'll die if you don't! Why me? Why am I being chased by a crazy man with a knife? Can't keep this up! Can't! Should I just have let him stab me earlier? If I hadn't run. If I'd stayed still.

He'd have stabbed me anyway. But at least it would've been over! I wouldn't have had to suffer this agony. Why did I run? My legs. Won't move anymore! All that dancing earlier. Oh somebody help me! Please someone help me. I turn around and he's only five yards away. He's gonna catch me. What am I gonna do? What am I gonna do? What'm I gonna do! The main street is just in sight. I see three office workers waiting for a cab. I scream as loud as I can: 'HELLLPPPP! Oh help me! Help me! If you help me I'll be your slave! I'll serve you the rest of my life! I really mean it!'

4

15th Winter

'I'm not going home.'

'But it's already past your curfew.'

'That's exactly why I don't want to go home.'

'But that's just going to make them more angry.'

'Then come with me, Kitty.'

'But that's just going to get you into more trouble.'

'Then I'm not going home.'

'Listen, I'm going over to Hiro's house, so why don't you come by later, Rin?'

'OK . . .'

I peck him on the cheek, wave at him, and start off in the direction of my house. And when I turn around just once, there it is – a severed head impaled on the fence of Mr Suzuki's home. What a strange, strange sight. The man I love so dearly waving at me with a dead head just behind him. How long has it been since I first started seeing severed heads? As a child, I occasionally caught a glimpse of some hazy object, but as I grew older the object came into focus as a severed head. Or at least I think that was the way it was, but in reality I can't be sure. Maybe it just appeared one day. That's how the story can go. To me, the process of how I came to see it isn't important. It's not as if it does anything to harm me or causes me any real problems. It's just like it's a part of the natural flow of things. It's just become a part of my system.

I always do what Kitty says. Not just today, but always. No matter how convinced I am that I'm right, I do as he says. What Kitty believes is right, becomes my standard. If only I could escape with him and be with him forever instead of making my way home past my stupid curfew.

Clunk! The door makes a dull noise and a taut jolt passes from the handle and up my arm. I peer through the four-inch opening and try to see inside the house, but it seems like no one's home and all I can see is my cat Doma staring up at me curiously. But surely someone must be there if the chain is on. It's not as if my stupid little Doma could put the chain on. But this gives me an idea and I beckon him to come over. As I slide my hand into the gap and wave my fingers, Doma gets ready to hunt. He shuffles his back feet and seems ready to pounce any second and I plan to slowly move my fingers up the doorframe so that he'll jump up at the chain. But as soon as my fingers reach about waist height, Doma shoots me a look that seems to say, 'No way. That's outside my jurisdiction.' Then he shuffles around to turn his back to me. I try the doorbell and the home phone too, but there's still no response, so I glance up at the light coming from my father's room for a while before giving up and leaving through the front gate. They should know by now that there's always a good reason when I miss my curfew. I really didn't expect them to react with these extreme measures.

Although they are grown adults, Dad and Mum seem to lack endurance. But for me, endurance is what my life is all about. It's what has enabled me to live through the fifteen years and few months up until now. I basically need to endure every moment of my life except for those moments I spend with Kitty. In fact, even the moments I spend alone are moments I feel I have to endure. It doesn't matter whether I'm just sitting on the sofa in a daze, texting a friend, sitting at my desk reading or studying, or even just smoking a cigarette – everything requires endurance and I hate everything. But, of course, I still do these things. Because a world with Kitty is one worth living in. Until I met Kitty, I had practically no reason to live. I was beginning to get so fed up with my silly life in which living equalled enduring. I'd look at a dog and imagine it biting me to death or light a cigarette and imagine myself as a ball of fire or look up at the sky and imagine an airplane colliding into my skull. I'd think it was funny if I dropped my chopsticks. No, I wouldn't. I'd see chopsticks and imagine them rammed in my throat. Ever since I started at elementary school, I always seemed to be imagining my death. I'd imagine my home-room teacher murdering me and then I'd stop going to school. I'd imagine my corpse hidden inside the piano and then stop going to piano lessons. I'd imagine being gang-raped and killed in front of my mother and then I'd avoid seeing her. What a pain I was. But all that changed when I met

Kitty and I learned to be free from endurance. I'd never known of a place where endurance wasn't necessary, but meeting him allowed me to entrust myself to a feeling of freedom. What a pathetic, sentimental girl I am.

'Please come get me right now! I'm going to cry!'

Unexpectedly, I fly into a fit and these words spill out from my mouth. Yes, 'these words', not 'these thoughts'. That's more accurate, because thoughts can only exist in myself, so what meaning could thoughts have in a social context when they belong only to me? Surely they have no value at all. But since I don't think in terms of a social context, it might be correct to have said 'these thoughts' after all. But in the end it doesn't matter. I'm just a girl who needs Kitty to come and pick her up right away, right now, or she'll cry. It's not a matter of right or wrong.

I walk to the main road crying, and when I reach the intersection I sit crying under the lights of the pedestrian crossing and wait for Kitty. Not five minutes later he arrives and finds me sobbing and he strokes my hair.

'I got locked out.'

'And nobody let you in?'

'Why is it always, always me that gets treated like the bad one? Everyone else just does as they please and puts their own feelings first. But I'm the only one who always has to endure everything. So why should I be treated like the bad one! It's just cruel. Everyone's so cruel!'

'Don't cry.'

Kitty helps me to my feet and I squeeze his hand. Then he hugs me in silence. I sigh to myself and imagine what would happen if a clown were to mow us down in his van while rushing to a morning circus performance. Would he step out of the van to see our two dead bodies entwined? Would he climb on top of our fatal embrace and start to ride us like a ball? Would our entangled bodies start to roll down this asphalt road? The clown's colourful outfit is way too bright. Hey clown, don't worry, nobody would blame you. Nobody would hold you responsible for killing two people in the midst of happiness. And even if you did go to jail, you'd still be popular because you're a clown.

We manage to make it to Hiro's apartment without anyone running us down. Hiro has the face of a Hiro. I mean, the name fits his long face perfectly. His 'Ha-haha' laugh is uniquely characteristic of him. His only other distinguishing feature is the keloid scar on his left cheek that he got from a cigarette burn. I don't know if someone did it to him or if he did it himself. All I know is that the scar makes all of his expressions look foolish.

While realising that I shouldn't think that a person's foolish just because they have a foolish face, I can't help but feel that the foolishness does, however, come from that scar. In fact, when Kitty first introduced Hiro as a friend of his from playing mah-jong, I was so distracted by the scar that I couldn't offer him a proper hello. That's the kind of strength his scar possesses.

I sit smoking a cigarette and watching Kitty and Hiro play TV games. Hiro puts a beer out for me, but it isn't chilled. I place my knees under the coffee table and look at my reflection in the small mirror stood on the edge. My curls are falling loose, so I crumple my hair to make them tighter, then I focus on the sticker at the edge of the mirror. The character in the game Kitty and Hiro are playing is printed on it and I think how Hiro has some pretty childish interests for a 24-year old. But then, if I say that, then I guess you could say that someone who has visions of their own death on a daily basis is every bit as childish. Not so much because I have visions of death per se, but it's the specific visions I have – being run down by a clown, being eaten by some savage beast belonging to an animal tamer or plunging to my death after being forced to walk a tightrope. Surely someone who imagines such things can't be considered a grown-up. But what is a real death? Breathing my last in my old age on a hospital bed? Being crushed in a car accident? Being stabbed by some random street killer? At least I feel like I'll never die like that. Why? Well, because that's not the way I envision it. And as I never tell anyone about my visions, no one can ever interfere with the imaginings of my death. Although there may be some who might disagree with my take on this.

'Why don't you play too, Rin?'

Hiro must have noticed that I look bored. I wonder if that long vertical face would fit into this mirror and without looking away from the mirror I reply, 'No thanks.'

'That's because she sucks at this,' I hear Kitty say. But I don't suck and for a second I consider standing up for myself. But then I decide it's all so silly and close my mouth. I do suck at playing games actually, and standing up for myself isn't going to make me a better player, though I don't really want to become a better player anyway. The only reason why I'd considered standing up for myself is because I like the thought of appearing cute by saying it. But it's too late now to act cute, because my wrist is already covered with scars, and Kitty and Hiro both know that.

I often add a little 'yeah' at the end of my sentences. I do it even though I know people find it annoying. So why do I do it and try to act cute? It's because I like myself when I do. I slur my words, act stupid and call out 'Kitty!' like a child, because I like myself when I act that way. But when I'm alone, that's not how I act. I speak assertively and logically to a certain extent, and I know his name isn't Kitty. So what I'm saying is that I create a fake persona for my own satisfaction. Sometimes I get sick and tired of myself for doing it. And as a girl with cuts all over her wrists I know that I'll never really be cute no matter what I do. But in a way, I feel my life has become easier for me to live as a result of me not being cute. In the world I live in, it's more convenient for me to be seen as a pathetic girl. So, for that reason, I always make sure to have visible scars on my wrists. Actually, that's a lie, but I want all the people in the world to understand that this is my stance.

I kill my cigarette in the ashtray and there's some crackling and an unpleasant smell. There are strands of head hair and pubic hair in the ashtray and I imagine Hiro must have done a quick clean up before we came. It reminds me of a few years back when I went to a friend's house to play mah-jong and found a pubic hair stuck between the mah-jong blocks. I wonder how many thousands of pubic hairs a human being would have to swallow to die? Or would someone survive no matter how many they swallowed? Or maybe they'd die from getting them stuck in their throat. Or maybe the pubic hair would get tangled up with the vital organs and cause some sort of internal event. It'd be such a ridiculous way to die. One of the many ways to die that I admire. So from now on, maybe I'll collect all the pubic hair I find on my futon. But one thing is certain. The only pubic hairs I'd ever swallow would be Kitty's or mine.

At seven the next morning, Hiro calls out to us, 'The key's in the post,' and he leaves for work. Kitty and I go on sleeping until noon, and when we eventually wake up in the light that shines through the bed-sheet curtains, we have sex. It feels good to have sex in someone else's room. It's like we've conquered that place. We've had sex in all different sorts of places. My first time was from behind, with my hands clasped on to the slide in a park. There's nothing I like more than sex. And from the very first time I had sex, I've always placed great importance on it in my life. In fact, the most blissful moments in my life are ones when I'm having sex with Kitty.

It's past noon now. I'm suddenly overcome with an anxiety attack in Hiro's room. I end up going home in tears. I've left my pill case at home, so I don't have my pills. When I tell Kitty in sudden tears, he tells me to go home. But as soon as I realise myself that I don't have the pills, I'm subconsciously aware of the necessity to do so anyway. I'm incapable of living a normal life without pills. I don't think the dependency on pills itself is such a bad thing. It's just that without pills I can't lead a normal life, and the same goes for alcohol, cigarettes and sex. But in situations like this, I can't help but despise my dependency.

After separating from Kitty at the same place as yesterday, I go home and open the door just as I did the night before and it makes the same sound. I ring the door-bell, I bang on the door, kick it, throw my bag at it, throw small rocks through the gap, but there's still no response. I feel myself being overwhelmed by the anxiety that's normally kept under control by my pills and I feel a growing sense of irritation.

'Open the fucking door! Are you trying to kill me? I'll call the fucking cops!' And as I shout and kick the door, with the chain still on, it opens slightly and my mother's concerned voice says, 'You're being a nuisance to the neighbours.'

'Mum. Please just let me get my pills. I'll leave as soon as I get them,' I say tearfully, then my dad's voice echoes from inside.

'Don't open it,' he says.

So it seems that Dad is the one who's pissed off and I feel annoyed at how he hardly ever showed any interest in his children, but gets so enraged if I stay out past my curfew.

I stick my foot in the door like an aggressive salesman, reach my hand through the gap and say in a small voice that I hope only my mother will hear, 'Please, just my pills!'

The space between her eyebrows crimples. That's why she's so ugly. The photos I've seen of Mum when she didn't have such wrinkles were cute. Not even a trace of that cuteness is left in her now and such facts of the past have absolutely no meaning.

'I need to ask your dad.'

I hear Mum hurriedly muttering and realise that this is all futile.

'Give me my fucking pills you bitch or I'll kill myself today! Then it'll all be your fault, you child murderer!'

Images form in my mind. Me dying an unnatural death in a garden no bigger than a cat's forehead. Me dying by being impaled on a fence. Me swinging from a rope around my neck tied to the drainpipe. Many images flash through my mind and I wonder if I'm going to die because of these people. But why should I? Ever since I was born I've been used as an excuse not to get divorced, and all I lived for was for them to take advantage of me in any way they could. Shouldn't they pay me at least a little respect? I turned your sperm and your egg into something profound! I took your worthless semen and egg that were destined to end in a toilet tissue and turned them into this wonderful body. And it's all thanks to the fact that I continued to eat food and continued to crap and piss – all of my own will. So why this attitude towards me? But even if I were to say things like that, you guys would simply reply, 'You grew up on the money we earned and under our sanctuary.' To say such a thing is a parent's logic – and to say that I turned your worthless egg and sperm into what I am now is my logic. So there's no doubt that even if we were to talk about it, we'd never reach agreement. And I don't care to take part in pointless arguments. Anyway, arguments like that are no fun. And even if I were to add a bit of humour to the argument, my point still wouldn't go across. I've had many talks with adults over the years, but not once was I able to get through to them.

So I decide to take the most effective action I know to make them open the door. I cry endlessly, I yell and I scream, and perhaps it's because she considers the nuisance I'm being to the neighbours, my mother grapples to unlock the chain without waiting for Dad's permission. I burst open the door, push her to one side and walk into the living room. I'm certain I left my pills somewhere in the room, but I don't see the case anywhere – not on the sofa or the table or the chair, or even on top of the cupboard. Dad comes in and glares at me. But what good is that going to do? Why doesn't he just hit me? If I piss you off, then just hit me! I know you can't you raise your hand to a child. I look back at him with disdain and when I try to go to my room where my stock of pills is, he blocks me with his hand.

'Are you guys trying to kill me? You murderers. Aaaargh, fuck! You're killing me. Why don't you go kill yourselves instead?!'

As I shout my body starts to tremble. Whether it's because I haven't gone without my pills for a while or from despair, I don't know. But in any case, I tremble in a way that makes me think I might crumble at any moment.

'Why don't we just give her the pills, and let her leave?' Mum suggests. I like the way that my mother isn't stubborn and always gives in when there's about two steps left to go. Yes, yes, just do as you're told and hand me the pills. Otherwise I'll kill you both. I've always hated you guys, so it would be a great opportunity for me. Do you understand? I'll kill you. No. That's a lie. I don't kill. I can't despise anyone to the point that I'd kill them. I lost that drive a long time ago. I'm envious. Of people who can feel enough hatred to kill someone. Where does such determination come from? I don't understand. If I had such drive, I'm sure that even I could live more positively.

'No.'

The abruptness of this word from my normally kind and good-tempered Dad, shocks me. How? Why? If you keep this up, then I really might have to kill you! I don't hate you, Dad. But to protect myself, to get my pills, I might have to. It won't be a murder with positive consequences, like a murder that's driven by vengeance or done as a new experience. It'll be much less worthy than that. It'll just be for the sake of my pills. For the sake of myself.

Groaning, I bend my body until it's almost folded in half.

'Give me the pills, you bastard!' The yelling instantly drains my strength. 'Please, give me my pills.' The muttering increases my anger. 'I said give me my fucking pills, I'll fucking kill you!' I yell my strength away again. 'Please, give me my pills – have mercy on me!' I mutter and bring my anger back.

Mum looks like she can't stand it any longer and walks off to the kitchen. Seeing her, Dad bellows at her to stop. In an instant, I pick myself up and run to the kitchen where she's standing and I throw her aside and open the cabinet at the tip of her fingers. The entire stock that's meant to be in my room is all here. I grab a handful of the little plastic bags, with a daily dose in each and push them under my camisole. One bag falls to the floor, so I pick it up and put in my mouth, then I dash out again. Dad grabs my wrist at the front door, but I know he'd never put his hand under my camisole.

'Why can't you just abide by the rules?'

His angry voice is tinged with sadness and with his face all stiffened from so much anger I almost expect him to burst into tears. What would I do if he were to start crying? In that moment both Mum and I would be at a complete loss. But I've never seen Dad's tears, and it's hard to imagine I ever will. Mum always cries, but that's usually because of one of Dad's affairs. Dad, who doesn't cry, makes Mum cry. Maybe, Mum is crying for Dad. But why? No, Mum would never cry for Dad. Mum is Mum, and Dad is Dad. And even if they live together, they'll never become one. That's a very sad thing, because I intend to stay with Kitty forever, and one day we will become one. But seeing these two, who have already spent so many years together, haven't become one yet, it makes me doubt the possibility of my own wish coming true. I grunt through the plastic bag in my mouth. Mum is crying. I'm sick and tired of seeing her tears. I don't like her tears. When I was young, Mum cried often. I'm sure she must have been crying over Dad's affairs, but a small child doesn't have the complex emotional system that allows it to sympathise with a woman who's been cheated on. This is why I've always wondered about the emotional mechanism of a woman when being troubled by my mum's tears and hysteria. No, that's a lie. I was never troubled by her tears or hysteria. Although I did constantly worry whether she would take her frustration out on me – and whether she would be able to prepare dinner.

Why am I so full of lies? I should at least be able to be honest with myself when I'm alone, but apparently I'm not. So why am I this cynical? When my eyes catch those of a stranger, I feel like all my thoughts are transparent and known to them. So whenever that happens, I often think about weird things on purpose.

For example, if my eyes meet those of someone in front of me on a train, I think of an old man thinking, *Perhaps*

I should have lemon instead of milk in my iced tea, since I have rugby practice tomorrow, but actually no, I'll actually have iced coffee with cream, as he takes a seat on a park bench, and then finds a snake and sprains his back, but he doesn't own a mobile phone to call for an ambulance and dies a strange death as a result, and how a child watches him while holding an iced tea – or was it iced coffee? – in one hand. Those are the kind of thoughts I think.

If, while crossing the road, my eyes meet those of the driver of a car who's waiting for the lights to go green, then I sigh and think of how I have to do my homework when I get home, and how if I don't finish it I'm going to get a recorder shoved up my snatch. I think of how I'd plead for some lubrication and how my teacher would get offended by this and shove a piping-hot sausage up my snatch instead. But actually he doesn't shove it up and instead starts huffing and puffing on it, so I think he's going to eat it. But then, before he bites into it, he smears fresh cream on his lips. But hold on – it's not a regular sausage at all. 'It's a chorizo!' he says in shock and glares at me. Those are the kinds of things I would think.

This habit of thinking of strange things on purpose is something I feel I should do something about one of these days. But the idea of consciously controlling subconscious thoughts is ridiculous. If I did that, I'd probably lose what was good about me, too. So my intention to do something about it someday is probably a lie. I like the way I think these strange things.

Hearing a scraping noise, I look up from the front door to see Doma clinging on to the pot on the landing. I wonder why, but the moment I think that, the pot falls over with a crash and sends Doma flying. He'd probably fallen from the handrail and had been clinging on to the pot for dear life. While Mum and Dad look at the pot that's cleanly broken in half, I tear the plastic bag that's covered with my saliva and swallow the four pills inside. My hands and face are hot and covered in tears and saliva, so I look like I've just stepped out of the bath. I feel the other bags tucked up under my camisole, brushing and tickling against my bare breasts.

'Would you guys rob me of my morphine if I was dying of cancer? Can't you acknowledge the fact that I'm doing my best to maintain some level of control while suffering from my disorder? Do you think I'm faking this and tricking the doctor into giving me the pills?' Though they've calmed down, I accuse them both to their faces. But they ignore me and just say what they want to say. Whatever happens, you must come home by midnight. You need to stop breaking your curfew almost every day. Stop going to clubs and games arcades and stop fooling around with your boyfriend. I've had meaningless talks like this in home-room at school, and like there I nod my head now and again, while picking at my nails.

By the time I've picked all the varnish off my little finger and forefinger, I'm finally set free and allowed to go back to my room. I throw my bag on the sofa and call Kitty.

'I took my pills,' I tell him, and he says, 'That's a relief' and 'I decided to go to university, since I haven't been in a while.'

I whine that I want to see him right away, but he says he'll come see me as soon as classes are over. I reluctantly consent. I don't go to school right now, but my entrance to high school has already been decided. When I graduate from middle school I'll enter high school. I've often thought that a girl's life is over at sixteen. But this summer I really will turn sixteen. So from now on I'll believe that a girl's life is over at eighteen. I'll think that way. Because I don't feel at the moment that I'm finished and it's hard to think I'll be over in another six months. At sixteen, I can get married. Someday I'm certain I'll get married to Kitty.

I sit on the edge of the window, stretch my hands over to the desk and grab my cigarettes. As I inhale the smoke, I feel like my entire body has turned a smoky colour. Like I'm being smoked. I feel like it's getting murky in here and I open the windows, and I end up breathing in smoke and cold air at the same time. I'm straining the muscles between my brows and I wonder why. Sometimes, I feel like everything I am thinking or doing or believe in, is being laughed at by somebody. Then I look up out of my window at the sky and see a severed head on top of the telephone pole. The slain samurai staring silently at me with dead eyes. I wave my hand slightly, but he doesn't smile or wave back as he's got no hands. Poor thing. Should I feel sorry for the samurai? Or should I feel sorry for myself, because I can't climb up a telephone pole? Should I feel sorry for myself that I'm sitting on the window ledge staring at the poor samurai? Or for the samurai staring at poor me smoking on the window ledge? What was the object of pity here? The way our gazes crossed? The sight of us from the sky? Or the sight of us from someone down on the street? Hey, slain samurai, what's the correct answer? I question him with my eyes, and I notice I'm lying again. There actually isn't anything to feel sorry for. I simply want to feel sorry for something.

Playing poker with Kitty, Hiro and Akito, I win 2,000 yen. With that money I buy a pregnancy test with two testers and I pee on one in a public toilet. Some pee gets on my hand, but I pay it no mind. I place the tester on top of the toilet-paper holder and wipe my hand and private parts with strong toilet paper. I wait one minute with my panties still down and squatting, then I compare the sign that appears with the one on the instructions. I see me dying with my head in the toilet, me choking to death from swallowing toilet paper, oh, and I totally forgot to collect pubic hairs! I think of this and that, and in the end I'm locked up in the toilet for about five minutes. But, as all people who enter the toilet do, I eventually leave. I hand the tester to Kitty, who is waiting for me on the bench. I tell him I'm pregnant, then I fall to the ground sobbing.

Kitty immediately sits me down next to him and compares the tester and instructions, just as I did only moments ago. The fact that the tester that I've just sprayed urine on is now in Kitty's hand gives me a strange feeling. The moment I saw the positive sign, I thought that I wouldn't be able to think anything at all. But the fact that I can think *The tester I peed on is in Kitty's hand* makes me disgusted with my own selfishness. *The tester I peed on is in Kitty's hand, in Kitty's hand, in Kitty's hand*. But actually, I couldn't give two shits about that. He's seen me peeing before and I've even sprayed some pee on him before. Peeing is something that I don't think needs to be awkward.

I don't want to see it. I don't want to have to face a world where there's a baby in my belly. But I have to see it. I never knew there could be a world so difficult to accept. A world so harsh. A world so completely different from the one in which I used to laugh at myself for spending all of my time daydreaming. It's a different world from the one in which I used to wonder to myself 'What world'? A completely different world from the one in which I used to joke to myself 'The world is that thing that lives in my vagina, isn't it?' The world that I'm looking at now is different from all worlds before in every respect. Until now, my worlds were worlds with severed heads in them. With Kitty in them. And they were the only worlds I knew. I chose to live only in those worlds. Now, against my will, I'm being pulled into a world where there's a tiny baby in my belly. It's as if I've been suddenly kidnapped, had my arms and legs cut off, and been sold as a meat slave. As if everybody on earth but myself has been brutally killed. As if I've been flown off to Mars without warning. Has Kitty realised the gravity of the situation? My eyes are blurred by tears that keep falling even as I wipe and wipe, so I'm unable to check his expression. Hey, Kitty. Kitty. I reach out my hand as if I've become blind, and Kitty takes it in his.

'It's not 100 per cent definite yet, right?' he says. 'Let's wait another couple of days, and take the test one more time.'

My eyes meet those of a middle-aged woman looking at us suspiciously. I'm crying. I'm crying because I'm pregnant and I don't know what to do, but I'm not going to let her find that out. So I think my thoughts.

I wonder why I started crying at the thought of going bald. I think of how I'd initially thought of collecting pubic hairs to make a wig, and how I needed to set out on an adventure, and by doing that we'd lost the elections, despite all the preparations that had gone into it. In the end, it's all about the money.

The warmth of Kitty's arm weakens me and all the thoughts that I never thought would stop come to an end. I turn my eyes away from the middle-aged woman and press my face against Kitty's chest. I think to myself, *Kitty, Kitty. What's going to happen? What am I going to do?* But I don't really want to ask those things. What I really want to ask is what Kitty wants to do. So why did I think of those other things? It's probably because I want Kitty to decide which path to take, and because I want to dump all the responsibility on him. I think that, but I don't accept it. I don't accept things I don't want to. That's what I've always done. But this time I feel that's not going to work. Even then, I can't accept it. I plan to somehow escape from this world. Even though I know such a thing isn't possible. Such a thing? Yes. I want to escape so badly.

Two days later, in the toilet of my house, I take the test a second time. I take the tester, with its positive mark, back into the room and when I hand it to Kitty, we both lapse into silence. For two days I've stayed off my pills, which I never believed I could do. But so far, I haven't lost control or been attacked by sudden desperation, anxiety or fear. Perhaps the part of me that depended on the pills is now depending on the baby in my belly instead. Yes, I've noticed. I too am already beginning to depend on the baby in my belly. But this makes no sense. Pills bringing my emotions back to stability or controlling my depression – that makes sense. But there's no way a baby can stabilise my emotions or control my depression. I must have known that it is much too early to start using my baby as a tool for comfort like my mum and dad did.

'I want to graduate from university.'

'What are you talking about?'

But by the time I've said 'what', I've already figured out what he's talking about. Basically, Kitty wants me to have an abortion. So why did I add the rising intonation for 'about' at the end? Because I didn't want to understand. I didn't want to accept it, that's why. I'm always full of pointlessness. I continue to think and speak pointless things. If I hadn't added the word 'about', then I could have talked with Kitty about something else for the duration of that wasted word. But thinking this pointless thought is, in itself, pointless.

'I want to at least graduate from university.'

'What do you mean 'at least'? Do you mean you want to graduate from university for now?'

There I go, pretending not to understand again. I'm not making any sense – 'at least' and 'for now' are like synonyms in a case like this. To know that Kitty wants me to abort the child should be enough, but instead I push my finger deeper into my wound. I scratch my flesh with my sharpened nails, then I dig my nails in and claw at my fat, and I keep stretching the tear in my skin as if trying to gouge something out. But nothing will come out. I know that.

'I want to graduate.'

'Why? You said we should have the baby if I got pregnant. Why? Was it a lie?'

What a cliché. I never thought I'd say such pathetic words, like a woman with no style. I don't want to say those words. But isn't it strange how Kitty had previously told me to have the baby if I got pregnant? Why would he lie? Again I'm pretending like I don't know. But really it's not surprising at all. Just imagine if I were in his shoes. He'd probably just said it to make me happy, or so he could have unprotected sex with me. Or maybe it was both, or maybe he really thought he wanted me to have the baby, but then when it became a reality he got scared.

Either way, it must be some ridiculous reason like that. And for whatever ridiculous reason it is, Kitty has decided that he wants to graduate from university. I thought a person's psychology would be more complex than that. But is it really? Isn't it rather simple instead? I don't accept such complexity. I don't accept this complexity that will lead to the killing of another person.

'Of course the decision is up to you, Rin. But I can't take the responsibility.'

'What? That's horrible.'

That's just . . . so harsh! I know that somewhere inside I'm relieved at being given a reason to have an abortion, and that I'm accusing Kitty to hide my relief. I see me dying from shouting at him, until my throat bursts into flames. Me dying of dehydration through crying too many tears. Me going into shock and starving to death. I imagine such things and I'm unable to think of anything. So taking advantage of this, I purposely fall into silence to achieve a moment of peace. Kitty's face appears in the corner of my sight. And as I'm leaning forwards while sitting down, his face is all that I can see – just another severed head. But the world is made of severed heads. Even trees, when they're dug up, they have a severed head at their roots, and even cars are made from misshapen bones of severed heads, and even nail varnish is made by melting the brains from severed heads, and even books are made from the skin of severed heads. Why do I think that everything is a severed head? What benefit is there for me in doing so? Perhaps I want to think that the value of the world is, at times, equivalent to that of a severed head. So if the value of the world really were equivalent to that of a severed head, then what sort of benefit would that hold for me? If that were the case, would I be able to go on laughing and living?

'Whether you decide to have the baby or to abort it, you still have to go to the hospital, at least once.' The words coming from this severed head make me twitch and I turn around to see that Kitty isn't a severed head any longer. This thing that was, until moments ago, a severed head is now a normal human again. I freeze for a moment in this first experience. Or at least I pretend to. In fact, I don't feel any hesitation at all and I know everything that has just happened is the obvious way for things to turn out.

Together, we go downstairs to the living room and tell Mum, who's washing the dishes, that we have something to say. When Kitty tells her about the pregnancy, she rests her elbows on the table and tries to hide her devastation . . . or her devilish grin – I can't be sure, as both her hands cover her face. Suddenly she pulls herself together, says, 'You'll have to have an abortion,' and she calls for Dad.

No. Don't tell Dad. I don't want Dad to know. If Dad finds out about my pregnancy, he might make that sad expression again, like he did when he shouted at me.

'She says she's pregnant. She'll have to have an abortion.' Mum's clear voice. She looks at me as if she's shining with the arrival of a purpose in life and the moment I see that I feel nauseous. I feel both fear and relief at the thought of my future being decided by another person. I have to say something. Have to say what I think. Have to assert myself. I have to tell them what *I* want. Or I could just offer an opinion. Something. Even if it's only one word, I need to say something about how I feel about the pregnancy. Otherwise it will be no different from the times they took advantage of me as a tool for comfort when I was a baby. Then things will be no different from the times when I asserted nothing. When I existed to serve as a tool of comfort for them. When I was nothing more than a cheap commercial product. I'm not your sperm and egg. I'm not a sperm and egg. I'm a whole girl who produces her own eggs every month. That's why I'm pregnant. I'm no longer just a sperm and egg.

'Well, I guess that's the only option. If that's the way it is, then that's what will have to be done,' says Dad, matter of fact. He looks neither sad nor mad, he doesn't seem to find the idea painful, he doesn't seem to struggle with the issue; he just speaks with a slight frown.

Why, Kitty? Why, Mum? Why, Dad? I question them all without speaking a word.

I am a sperm and egg. No, wait. It's not just me. Every single person living in this world is a sperm and egg. I'm just like everyone else. I'm no different from everyone else. But nonetheless it seems I'm inferior to other people. Having spoken his part, Dad leaves the living room without meeting my eyes.

'Let's go to the hospital tomorrow.' And with Mum's words, the talk ends.

I sit with my legs up on the chair and glare at the table. I've been in this position forever. The markings of the wooden table burn into my eyes; the black, round patterns like the eyes of an animal, like a solar eclipse. What am I doing, drawing connections between my abortion and the universe? Kitty and Mum stare at me as I sit with my head down in silence. I'm supposed to go to the hospital now, but I'm stubborn. I've always been stubborn. I even used to dread going to kindergarten and I used to cry every single day. And when they forced me to go, I felt like I'd been dropped off at a different world and I cursed everything I saw there. I remember the tears and the tantrums. After kissing Dad goodbye on the cheek, I'd remember the sight of him waving his hand and leaving the house and it would make me cry. I'd always be thinking about Dad when I cried at kindergarten. But by leaving time I'd have become friends with the other kids and I'd be thinking of it as a fun place. But then the next morning, I'd be thinking of it as hell all over again. Then I'd remember Dad and cry, then I'd think of it as a fun place again. So which was it really? I don't know. Perhaps hell is a fun place and even fun places can be hell, or perhaps hell is turning into a fun place day after day. I'm stubborn. I remember the face of my mum as she used to drag me to kindergarten, while I refused to move my legs. Back then I'd hated her so much that I could have killed her. I would imagine stabbing a pair of scissors into her neck or pouring mercury down her throat. 'You'll die if you drink mercury,' she used to say to scare me when she placed a thermometer under my armpit, whenever I'd feigned sickness to get a day off from kindergarten. But I no longer have the hatred in me needed to kill another human being.

Mum and Kitty take me to the women's clinic, but I collapse to the ground ten yards from the door. I rub my cheeks on the asphalt, I cry and I scream, and I stay that way until the clinic closes. Mum is angry. Kitty hugs me. And the pasta carbonara with cheese I have that night tastes like the most delicious thing on this earth.

The next day I go with Mum again for my examination and my pregnancy is confirmed. Mum asks to set a date for an abortion right there and then. I go home and lock myself in my room, where I pull Doma up on to my lap and play with the undersides of his paws. I tell him what's happening in cat language. 'There's a baby inside here. It's even smaller than you.' I press his paws on my stomach and Doma turns his body around, cuddles up against me and replies with a meow. I stroke his soft fur as he falls asleep on my stomach and I lean against the window. A severed head has fallen onto the roof of the Satos' house across the street. *Shit!* I think to myself, but then I remember that the severed heads are really nothing to do with me and I breathe out a lungful of air. The severed head doesn't roll about on the roof tiles or fall to the ground. Instead it lands and remains on the highest point of the roof with the top of its head facing the sky. The slain samurai is staring at me today, too. I feel my sense of calm ebbing away and I cry, cry and cry

207

as the slain samurai and I stare at each other. I feel like I could cry without ever stopping. Doma wakes up to my crying and climbs off my lap looking slightly perturbed. I keep on crying with my arms wrapped around my knees and my shoulders, rocking with an occasional glance at the severed head.

'It seems that the heart is beating.'

It's only when the doctor says this that I realise how the heartbeat belongs not to me but to the baby. My doctor for the abortion has a kind face. But the fact that it's someone with a kind face telling me that makes me hang my head.

'Please don't have anything to eat on the day of the operation. Sleep well the night before, and please don't drink any alcohol,' says the doctor. 'Sorry, I forgot you're under age!' She quickly laughs. I try to laugh back, but only one side of my lips turns up and all I can think is how disgusting the nurse standing by my side is. With my head still bowed I go into the waiting room where Mum is and even though I notice her, I can't make myself look her in the face.

On the way back, I send Mum home and go into the department store by myself. I go to the baby products section and buy a baby's rattle. There are plenty more things I want to buy, but I can't imagine that a soon-to-be aborted baby would appreciate them and it wouldn't make me happy either. I don't even know why I bought the baby's rattle, but somehow I felt that it was necessary.

But for who? For the baby? Or for myself? I know. It's for myself. The baby hasn't tried to indicate anything to me yet. From the way that I'm constantly hungry even after eating and eating, it seems like it at least wants to live, but there's nothing I can do to change its fate. This is where I stop my thoughts. I hate myself almost to the point of wanting to kill myself for stopping my thoughts here, but I can't do that. That's the me that lives in this world. *Just die.* Not the baby. Me. But even if I think that way, I still won't die. How pathetic. *Die.* But I won't. Why aren't humans made so that they can explode the very second they feel the will to murder themselves? I should die. Once home, I shake the baby's rattle and talk to my stomach. I give the baby a name and I write a letter to it. *You should fucking die.* I attack myself in my mind, knowing it'll only make the pain worse. I know this, but I continue to attack myself.

Kitty has stayed with me practically every day, but I can't open my heart to him anymore. When my eyes meet his I think of strange things again to hide what I'm really thinking. I find it silly how I'm acting self-conscious in front of someone who I've always wanted so badly to understand me. So whenever our eyes meet I find myself giving him a weird half-smile. 'I don't like watermelons because they have seeds, and the way that they have kind of a smell, you know? So I was thinking, why not put prosciutto on watermelon?' The woman saying that has packaging tape stuck to her breasts, for some reason, and it bothers me. But with my half-smile, I listen to her talking without ever knowing whether that tape got there on purpose or if it was an accident? I wonder if it's perhaps a homage to the melon, or an attempt to deny the *raison d'être* of prosciutto. I think how she's talking with the ocean to her back and perhaps there's a chance that I'm hearing her wrong, because of all the noise of the waves in the background. Or perhaps not? Or is she talking about water-melons, which I don't like, because she doesn't like me? So which is it? If I had to say one way or the other, which would it be? These are the thoughts I'm thinking.

When I arrive at the clinic with Kitty and Mum, I'm taken to a private room and told to change into a surgery gown. I'm told they're going to check the opening to my uterus, then I step up on to the examination chair and the doctor asks me, 'You don't want to see the ultrasound scan, do you?' And I shake the curtains in front of me that hide the parts of me below my chest.

'I do. Please show me.'

The doctor hesitates at first, but opens the curtains. And there it is, the baby. There, in fact, exists a baby in front of me. I question my very existence. I wonder if it isn't me who's going to be aborted in a short while? And while I'm still wondering, the doctor says, 'That should be enough' and closes the curtains. Then she takes me to the back room and I get up on to the operating table.

'I'm going to use an anaesthetic,' she tells me, and I see it going into my body through the needle. The nurse tells me to count, so I count seconds with her.

'One, two, three . . .'

How many seconds will it take for me to lose consciousness?

'Four, five, six . . .'

The fluorescent light in front of me gets blurry.

'Seven, eight . . .'

I feel like I can hear my own voice echoing in my head.

'Nine . . .'

No! I can't do it! A tear falls from my eye. I'm going to have the baby! I want to tell the nurse who is holding my hand! But the moment I turn my head towards her I lose consciousness. The last thing I remember is the sight of the fluorescent light on the ceiling reflected on the side of the table.

I awake lying down on the bed of a private room, and for a while I don't know what's going on. Oh . . . Oh no. My baby. I remember and place my hand on my belly, which feels the same as it always does. Perhaps the words I'd wanted to say – 'I'm going to have the baby!' – perhaps they'd been understood after all and the abortion itself had been aborted. I look around the room to try to understand my situation. Hey, is the baby in my belly or not? What's happening? What about my baby? I sit up and I notice that I'm wearing underpants that I've never seen before. I reach my hand down and feel a napkin pressed inside them. So it's really not there. There's no baby in there anymore. My baby is dead. It's gone. It doesn't exist now. I think these thoughts over and over. No, but it might still be here. It was here just a short while ago. Only two, three minutes ago.'

I notice a snack and some tea on the table by my pillow. I'm terribly thirsty and without thinking I pour some tea and gulp it down, but immediately my intestines seem to twist painfully and I double up holding my stomach. I try to get up to go to the toilet, but I don't make it that far and I throw up in the basin, where I continue to gag and cough up my stomach acids. My shoulders are shaking uncontrollably and a nurse runs in and with a panic-stricken face asks me what happened. I tell her that I drank some tea and then threw up and she leads me back to bed.

'Please, sleep a little more,' she tells me as she lays me down and tucks the covers over my chest. What happened to my baby? I want to ask her so badly. I have to check. I have to. But I'm so scared of the answer. But I can't stop myself from asking, so I turn to her.

'Ma . . . um . . . my ba . . . by?'

She seems to understand what I'm trying to say and she looks at me with pity. The moment I see her expression, tears start to fall one after the other. Choking and crying I hear the nurse tell me never to do anything like this again and with both my hands covering my face I just nod and nod again. After she leaves, I continue to cry while straining to keep my voice down. My baby's remains might still be in this hospital. I can't let it hear me crying. Because I killed it. My mind becomes hazy again and I fall back into sleep.

It's now been one week since I came home looking like death. One week into the relief of it all being over. One week after the horror of killing someone. I allocate most of my time during the day to observing the severed head. And when I can't find the severed head from my window, I just cry and cry. Life is endurance. My baby was lucky to die without knowing that sort of endurance. The moment I think that, I want to kill myself again. What the fuck am I thinking? Anyone who says such a thing, even as a joke, should be killed! Kill them all. Bring on the end of the world. *Just die.* The moment I think that, I see my own corpse. It's a baby that was never born – so you can't call that a life. So that means I couldn't have killed the baby. But the moment I say that, I want to kill myself again. What the fuck are you saying, bitch? For fuck's sake! In my mind, I see my own corpse again and the cycle starts over again. I don't kill myself. But what am I? I'm just a pain – a woman who can't even kill herself. So what the fuck am I doing thinking this over and over? *Just die!* I shake the baby's rattle and imagine my death yet again, and I cry and scream and shout, until I eventually fall asleep with what feels like my last breath.

Two weeks after the abortion Kitty starts to take me outside. The sight of me after I've spent every day endlessly going through the same old questions and self-recriminations and watching the severed head must have been a strange one for him. The people at the games arcade where we always went, at the fast food shop outside the station, at the taxi stand – they all have dead eyes. No, they don't even have eyes. But they're all dead anyway. No, they have the eyes of a fish. And they stink of fish. I try to tell Kitty this, but he just tries to comfort me and tells me it doesn't smell of fish; then he smiles uncomfortably. So if it doesn't smell fishy, does it smell like squid? I haven't had sex for a long time now. In fact, ever since I got pregnant, I haven't had sex once. So is this squid smell coming from Kitty's hand? From the hand he masturbated with? I sniff his hand, but I can only smell sweat. So where's the squid? *This squid-smelling world should be completely destroyed*! I try my best not to say these thoughts out loud. But after a while, the fact that I'm trying so hard to hold myself back seems silly and I wonder why I should do this. This thought pisses me off and in the end I blurt out that I just can't go on living in a world that smells of squid, and I start crying and Kitty takes me home.

Now I haven't even got the energy to take out my feelings on Kitty, so I just sit here watching the severed head. My cigarettes run out, so I reach for a new pack from the carton and notice it's the last one. I know that after I finish this pack I'm going to have to rip the plastic off the new carton and I imagine what a hassle that will be and just thinking about it makes me feel lethargic. While smoking my cigarette I unconsciously reach for another one. I think I want to smoke a cigarette when I'm already smoking one. 'Right then, I'll have a cigarette,' I think to myself and I take a cigarette from the pack only to notice there is a lit cigarette in the ashtray. I reach out for the cigarette in the ashtray, but as soon as I do, I realise there's already a cigarette held in my lips. The air in the room is stuffy and it constantly feels smoky. If I stay in a room where the air is as bad as this, someday something will go wrong with my respiratory system and I'll die. That's the plan anyway.

As April nears, I start to get anxious. On the first of April I start at a new high school. But I'm in no state to be going. The phone rings. I'm in no state to pick it up. But I do. Somewhere inside me I know that I have to do something on my own. I have to bring about a change in myself, by myself.

'Hello?'

'Oh, Rin? You answered finally!'

'Hiro?'

'Yeah. I haven't seen you around lately, so was wondering what you were up to.'

'Yeah, everything's going well.'

'What is?'

'Yeah . . .'

I know I'm not communicating. So what? You have a problem with that? Well it can't be helped. I'm a hopeless human being. So there's really no way I can make myself change on my own.

'Hey Rin, are you on drugs?'

'What? What's that?'

'Well, he said you're always fucked up these days, and it's hard spending time with you, so I was worried a little.'

'Who's "he"? Kitty?'

'Yeah. So are you doing drugs?'

'Yeah.'

'You are?'

'Yeah.'

I lied. But I accepted it all. I accepted the way Kitty was. My child's death. Myself. The fact that I couldn't make a decision for myself about whether to have the baby or to abort it. The fact that I'm still breathing despite my constant visions of my own death.

They told me not to have intercourse for one month after the abortion. So exactly thirty days later, I had sex with Hiro. Kitty soon found out and we broke up. Now, as I lean on the window ledge, I think, *I won't die, I definitely won't die, I won't die for the rest of my life. I'm deathless. The severed head won't fall and I can no longer even imagine that I would die. I'll make a change in myself, by myself. I know now that I can.*